HOUSEHOLD DEMONS

HEDGEWITCH FOR HIRE – BOOK 3

CHRISTINE POPE

Dark Valentine Press

HOUSEHOLD DEMONS

Copyright © 2021 by Christine Pope

ISBN: 978-1-946435-43-9

Published by Dark Valentine Press

Cover design by Lou Harper

Ebook formatting by Indie Author Services

Guess Who's Coming to Globe?

MY MOTHER'S VOICE PRACTICALLY VIBRATED with excitement. "Selena, I've got a surprise for you!"

I didn't bother to hold back my wince, since we were talking on the phone rather than having one of our occasional Zoom calls. While my mother was the most well-meaning person in the world, her "surprises" often turned out to be the sort of thing I would prefer to avoid. A year or so back, she'd finally abandoned all the various fix-ups with the sons of friends or friends of friends she kept trying to arrange for me, but I'd still learned to be wary whenever she decided to spring something on me out of the blue.

However, I tried to make myself sound moderately excited as I replied, "What surprise?"

"Well...." She drew out the syllable, as if

doing her best to prolong the suspense. But it seemed clear she couldn't restrain her enthusiasm for very long, because she followed that one word by exclaiming immediately, "We bought a house in Globe!"

"You *what?*" I blurted, too startled to rein in my response. "What about Tom's business?"

Tom McGill was my mother's husband. I suppose that technically made him my stepfather, but I never really thought of him that way, since he'd come on the scene when I was twenty-three and long out of the house. He was just as nice a person as my mother, so they were well-suited to each other. However, he'd owned his plumbing supply company in Tarzana for almost twenty years, and even though I guessed he was getting close to retirement age—he was twelve years older than my mother—I still couldn't quite envision him giving up a business he'd built from nothing, just to settle down in my sleepy little adopted hometown.

"Oh, we're not planning to live in Globe full-time," my mother replied at once, and a wave of relief flooded through me. It wasn't that I didn't love her or anything, but we'd been living fairly separate lives for a decade, and I didn't honestly know how I would have handled having her in my lap all the time.

"No," she went on, "Tom has been thinking

for a while that he'd like to buy another property, something we could stay in for a few weeks out of the year and then use as a vacation rental the rest of the time. I hear those Airbnb things are very popular."

"They are," I said cautiously, even as I reflected that of course she wouldn't know much about Airbnbs, because whenever she and Tom traveled, they stayed in five-star resorts and flew first class. You might not think there was a lot of money in running a plumbing supply company in the Valley, but my mother's husband had done very well for himself. "So, tell me about the house."

"Oh," she replied, her tone brightening even further, "it's this big, beautiful Victorian mansion at the top of a hill. The pictures made the view look incredible."

I'd only been living in Globe for a little more than four months by this point, but even I knew there was only one house in town which could possibly fit that particular description. "You bought the Bigelow mansion?" I asked, trying not to sound too incredulous and probably failing miserably.

"Yes," my mother said. "Josie's photos convinced us that it would be just perfect."

Josie Woodrow, Globe's foremost real estate agent…and someone I counted as a good friend. I couldn't believe she'd hidden the whole transaction from me, not the least because she was one of the biggest gossips I knew, and I didn't see how she'd managed to keep such a juicy secret.

But that was a lesser concern compared to the warning bells that had started to go off in my mind. "Mom, that place is totally haunted. Didn't Josie tell you that?"

"Oh, sure," she said, sounding as airy as Josie herself. "But you know I don't believe in that sort of thing."

Yes, my mother steadfastly continued to believe that the supernatural world was nothing more than the result of a bunch of people's overactive imaginations, including mine. I'd pleaded with her on more than one occasion to sit in on one of my crystal ball sessions with Grandma Ellen—my mom's late mother—but my mother had always steadfastly refused, telling me she didn't think it would be respectful.

I'd long since put aside my annoyance with her denial of all things supernatural, since it was her life and she needed to decide how she wanted to live it, but this was different.

"It doesn't matter whether *you* believe it or not," I told her. "The Bigelow mansion's hauntings are pretty well documented. The place was even featured on one of those cable TV ghost-hunting shows."

"No wonder it was such a hot property," my

mother replied. "We actually got into a bidding war over the place, which wasn't something we'd expected from a real estate transaction in Globe. But you know how Tom is when he gets his heels dug in. He wanted that house no matter what. So, we got it in the end."

I hadn't heard about that. But then, I didn't pay much attention to Globe's real estate market unless Josie was telling me about her latest listing, and clearly she'd held her cards close to the vest on this one. At the same time, I had to wonder who else had wanted the Bigelow mansion so badly they were willing to get into a bidding war with an out-of-state investor with deep pockets.

Then again, even the hottest property in Globe wasn't exactly going to run into millions. It wasn't like we were back in Southern California.

"That's great," I said, although I honestly wasn't sure how "great" this whole development would turn out to be. "When do you think you'll be coming to Globe?"

"Saturday," she responded immediately. "Tom wanted to finish out the work week and get some business wrapped up, but then we'll be out there to look over the place and stay for at least a week, maybe more."

Which meant I had three days before they showed up. I had to wonder what the two of them planned to do while they were in Globe. The place wasn't exactly known for its entertainment options, unless you were big on hiking. Tom liked to golf, and golf courses were in short supply in the area, although I supposed he could make the trek up to Payson to play. There were golf courses in the eastern Phoenix suburbs, of course, but playing golf in Queen Creek in early August didn't sound like much fun.

But my mother loved to putter in the yard, and I had a vague recollection that the grounds of the Bigelow mansion were fairly extensive, with a rose garden and several other points of interest, including a maze and an apple orchard. That might be enough to keep her occupied.

"Well, let me know when you get here," I said. "I'll show you around."

"Oh, of course!" she responded brightly. "I want to see your store in person…and I hope I'll get to meet this Calvin you've told me about."

Calvin Standingbear and I had been dating since the end of June. As July progressed and everything seemed to be going well between the two of us, I'd let slip to my mother that I was seeing someone local, although I hadn't gone into a lot of detail other than to tell her that my new significant other was the chief of the San Ramon tribal police, something she seemed to find impressive.

Obviously, I couldn't exactly tell her that

Calvin—and the rest of the San Ramon tribe—were a bunch of coyote shapeshifters.

"I hope so," I said, trying to sound vague. While it wasn't that I didn't want Calvin to meet my mother—and Tom—I had to wonder if this was too early in our relationship for the whole "meet the parents" thing. Although we hadn't done anything to hide the fact we were dating, I also couldn't help noticing that anything social we'd done had been in Globe itself, or over in Gilbert, where we'd gone wine tasting with Chuck Langdon and Hazel Marr, friends of ours who'd also started dating over the summer. Not once had Calvin taken me to dinner at the Gold Dust Casino, which the San Ramon Apache tribe owned and operated. In fact, the only time we spent on San Ramon Apache lands was when I went over to Calvin's house.

Was he trying to keep me away from his family, since the San Ramon tribe appeared to be very strict about its members getting involved with outsiders? The thought had crossed my mind more than once, but because Calvin and I hadn't been together all that long, I didn't want to get on his case about the situation. If things continued this way, maybe we'd have to have "the talk," although I hoped it wouldn't come to that.

At any rate, I had always thought I'd end up meeting his family long before he met mine, just because I'd never harbored even the faintest notion that my mother and Tom might want to live in Globe, if only for a few weeks out of the year. She'd never said word one about coming to visit me, even though I'd mentioned several times that I'd love to have her come if her schedule allowed. This lack hadn't really bothered me too much, since it had crossed my mind that even if she might have wanted to see the shop, she was waiting for a more opportune time of year. Everyone assured me that Globe was absolutely beautiful in the fall, and that seemed like a better time for a visit than late summer, even if the mythical monsoon storms had actually returned with a vengeance this year, filling up everyone's rain gauges and pretty much abolishing the word "drought" from the locals' vocabularies.

"Oh, I know your friend must be busy," my mother said. "It's so funny—I honestly never thought you were the type to get involved with someone in law enforcement."

On the surface, I suppose Calvin's and my relationship might have seemed a little odd, because a police chief hooking up with someone who ran a woo-woo New Age shop wasn't the sort of thing that happened every day. But, considering I was a witch and he was a shifter, it was actually a logical match in a lot of ways.

And even if it wasn't logical, I believed we'd be

together regardless. I knew I couldn't deny the chemistry we shared.

"Calvin's not your typical cop," I replied, and left it at that.

"Of course," she said quickly. "There's never been anything typical about you, Selena." Before I could attempt a response to that comment, she added, "Well, I need to run. Tom and I have a lot we need to get done before we head out on Saturday. We're driving, so we probably won't be there until late afternoon."

"That sounds good," I told her. "There's a fun little Mexican place here in town where we can all go to dinner."

"It's a date. See you Saturday!"

She ended the call then, and I pulled my iPhone away from my ear and set it down on the coffee table. Her call had come in while I'd run upstairs to my apartment to grab a quick lunch, and now I didn't have much time before the one o'clock return I'd set on my little "be back at" sign in the shop window made a liar out of me.

I'd have to eat lunch, and then head down and put in my afternoon shift in the store. After that, though...after that, Josie Woodrow and I were going to have a little talk.

"Well, of *course* I couldn't tell you anything," Josie said, making one of her trademark extravagant hand gestures. She sat behind the desk in her crowded pink-walled office, which was where I'd buttonholed her after closing Once in a Blue Moon a little early so I could catch her before she left work for the day. "I promised your mother that I would keep it a secret."

I crossed my arms. I'd taken a seat in the visitor's chair that faced her desk, but I'd perched on the edge rather than relaxing against the seat back. "No offense, Josie, but you're not exactly known for being able to keep secrets."

That remark made her shoot me a wounded look. "Of course I can…if it's important enough. Anyway, your mother was quite emphatic about wanting the house to be a surprise, so I put in an extra effort. Luckily, it was a very short escrow, since they were paying cash. I know it would've been difficult to keep the purchase from you if the transaction had stretched out for months."

I didn't know why I was surprised by that revelation. Tom McGill was a smart businessman, and I doubted he would want to go in debt over something that might turn out to be a boondoggle. If he and my mother ended up deciding that the house didn't suit them, he might not make a profit on its resale, but I had a feeling he'd at least be able to break even.

"And you told her about the ghosts?" I pressed, even though my mother had already come to Josie's defense on that topic.

"I certainly did," Josie replied, sounding wounded. She must have been to the salon recently, because her fiery hair blazed even more brightly than usual, making her pale blue eyes really pop. "I would never allow anyone to walk into that sort of situation blind...so to speak. She said she didn't believe in ghosts." That remark was accompanied by a small lift of an eyebrow, as if she was trying to figure out how the mother of a psychic could be so down to earth.

"She doesn't," I said. "My mother isn't much for the woo-woo stuff. Problem is, if the ghosts are there, they're going to do their thing no matter what she thinks."

"Oh, they're there," Josie said. Her brow creased slightly as she added, "Although, from all accounts, they're completely harmless. The previous owners said they moved small items around from time to time, and every once in a while there might be a random knock on the wall or a cold spot that came and went, but none of it interfered with their quality of life."

All of that did sound fairly innocuous, even if having your keys or your phone transported to another room might be annoying when you reached out for them and they weren't there. However....

"If the ghosts are so harmless, why did the former owners put the place up for sale?"

Josie shrugged. "It's a big place, and their children were grown and moved out. They're downsizing to a condo in Scottsdale."

Of course they were. Sometimes it felt as if the greater Phoenix metro area was a giant vortex, sucking everyone into it. Globe actually had slightly negative population growth, since a lot of the younger generation left to go to college and then never came back. Retirees liked to settle here because housing was inexpensive, but I supposed if you were sitting on a big, paid-for Victorian mansion, then the cost of living—even in Scottsdale—really shouldn't be an issue.

A thought occurred to me. Maybe my mother would view it as barging in where I hadn't been invited, but I considered it doing my due diligence. She didn't believe in ghosts. Fine. I did, and I wanted to know what my mother and her husband were walking into.

Besides, it was barely five, and Calvin wasn't expecting me at his place until seven, since he didn't get off shift until six-thirty. Plenty of time to go do an inspection.

"Okay," I told Josie. "I want to go see the house."

"Now?" she asked, looking startled.

"Yes," I said. "I've never been there. I want to get a sense of its vibes. You still have a key, don't you?"

"Of course," she replied. "I'm going to meet your mother and her husband there on Saturday to give them the keys and the remotes for the garage."

For some reason, I hadn't even thought about the place having a garage. It sounded like an utterly prosaic feature for a haunted Victorian mansion, and yet I knew that Tom would never have bought the house if it didn't have a space for his vehicles. He collected vintage sports cars, and he'd never leave one of his babies out in the sun and the weather.

"Well, then," I said. "Let's go take a look."

A-Haunting We Will Go

THE BIGELOW MANSION STOOD ON ITS OWN hill on the eastern edge of town, with spectacular mountain views on all sides. On the drive over—because Josie had insisted on bringing me in her Cadillac—she'd told me that the house had been built by the man who first found silver in these hills. His new wealth brought him a socialite wife from the East Coast, and she was the one who assisted in the design and decorating of their new home.

"It really is quite spectacular," Josie said as she pulled into the long gravel driveway. The garage was detached from the house, and probably had been built many years after the original construction. Even so, I could tell the architect had taken care to make sure it harmonized with the main structure, and the mansion's four-color paint scheme—dark brick red, forest and sage green, and pale gold—had been carried over there as well.

The mansion itself stood three stories tall and had a slate roof with a copper weathervane at its highest peak, along with a tower at the front and an expansive porch. No expense had been spared with the landscaping, either, as a broad green lawn with a flagstone path bordered in rosebushes swept you up to the front door, while the surrounding gardens were filled with flowers in full bloom as well as carefully groomed trees—willows and maples and sycamores. Off toward the rear of the property, I spied what I guessed was the apple orchard, its leaves glossy green in the August sun.

Even though I'd been expecting something impressive, I honestly hadn't thought the Bigelow homestead would be quite such an oasis in Globe's high desert. No wonder my mother had wanted the place—the gardens here would keep her busy for days.

"Definitely spectacular," I agreed.

Josie put her Cadillac in park, and we both got out and headed up the front walk. The air itself felt lusher here than it did down in town, filled with the scent of roses and fresh grass. From one of the trees in the backyard came the distinctive trill of a cardinal.

Josie wore a faint smile on her pink-lipsticked mouth, as if she could tell I was beginning to fall under the spell of the place as well. We climbed the steps to the front porch, and she fished a key with a plastic fob from out of her oversized purse.

"I really shouldn't be doing this," she said, although she didn't hesitate as she placed the key in the lock and turned it. "But since you're family, I suppose I'll let you and your mother work that out."

"I really don't think she'll mind," I replied, even as I mentally added, *Much.* "It makes sense to have someone check on the house before she gets here, after all."

This self-serving argument didn't appear to win me any points, since Josie only lifted an eyebrow. However, she went ahead and opened the door, and I stepped into the foyer.

Wow. The entry stood two stories high, and an enormous Tiffany-style chandelier hung from the coffered ceiling twenty feet above. Directly ahead was a huge sweeping staircase, while off to either side were what appeared to be parlors, both with oversized marble fireplaces and an impressive array of antiques of the same vintage of the house. All the original mahogany woodwork seemed to be intact, and the dark wood floor beneath my feet gleamed with the sort of gloss that could only be achieved with a whole lot of beeswax polish and elbow grease.

It all looked like something out of a movie. As impressive as the house was, though, I couldn't help contrasting it with the airy, Spanish-style home my mother shared with Tom back in Southern California. This place felt heavy and dark, very unlike my bright and cheery mom.

But maybe she planned to spend a lot of time outside while she was here, or possibly she just wanted her vacation home to be a complete change of pace. And I had to admit that this place would make a spectacular Airbnb—I could see people coming to Globe just so they could stay in a real honest-to-goodness Victorian mansion.

And that wasn't even including the ghosts.

Speaking of which….

I turned to Josie, who was standing a few paces away and watching me, clearly eager to see my reaction to the house. Since my mouth had dropped open a bit as we entered, I figured she already knew I was impressed by the place.

"Did you ever experience anything out of the ordinary while you were here?" I inquired.

She shook her head, looking almost regretful. "Not a thing. Hank and Nora—the previous owners—said it was probably because the ghosts were shy and didn't like to do much of anything around people they considered strangers, but I was still hoping I might see or feel something. But I didn't." A pause, and she slanted a curious glance up at me. "You don't feel anything, either?"

I hadn't yet, but that could have been because I wasn't actually trying. Since I wasn't a true medium, communing with the dead wasn't really my specialty. However, that didn't mean I couldn't give it the old college try.

"Let's find out," I said.

At random, I chose the parlor to the right and walked in that direction, making myself breathe quietly and rhythmically as I attempted to take in something of the mansion's energies. I thought that staying in the foyer probably wasn't a good idea, since most of the day-to-day activities in the house would have taken place somewhere other than the entry.

The walls here were papered with a pretty botanical print in muted shades of slate gray and burgundy. Normally, I wasn't a fan of wallpaper, but it suited the house and the furniture.

"All the furnishings conveyed with the house," Josie told me, maybe because she thought that information might help me with my ghost-hunting quest. "The previous owners wanted to make sure it would stay as it was while they lived here."

That was probably a good thing. After all, the place would lose a lot of its charm if someone tried to put modern furnishings in here. Also, if the mansion truly was inhabited by a couple of ghosts, the less disruption, the better. Some of the more spectacular hauntings I'd read about had been instigated by remodeling projects, or even simply redecorating a room or two.

And while I guessed it must have cost Tom and my mother a decent chunk to purchase all these antiques as well, doing so would save them the trouble of having a bunch of brand-new furniture shipped to Arizona.

"I'm going to try to sense if anyone else is here," I said. "I need to be quiet and focus."

What I really needed was for Josie to hold her tongue so I could concentrate, but I figured framing the situation this way was much more polite…not to mention having a better chance of success.

I walked a few more paces so I stood in the exact center of the room, then closed my eyes. Once all visual stimulus had been removed, I was more aware of other, subtler inputs—the faint smell of beeswax furniture polish, an even fainter hint of smoke from the huge marble fireplace…a drift of Chloé perfume from Josie's direction. A small creak from the floorboards as she shifted weight, another sharper creak that might have been the house settling.

Or maybe it was something else.

No, these all just felt like old house noises and nothing more. I didn't get a sense of anything else here other than Josie and myself, unless you could include the faint sounds of birds chirping in the garden. But nothing of an otherworldly presence, nothing that made me think this place could possibly be haunted.

Of course, she'd said that the Bigelow mansion's ghosts were shy and didn't like strangers. Maybe they were used to Josie, but they'd never encountered me before. They could be hiding.

Even so, I should've been able to get a hint of something. More than once in the past, I'd entered a house and known immediately that it had its own otherworldly residents, even if they weren't doing anything to manifest at the moment.

This place, though…it felt like a total blank.

"I'm not getting anything," I said, knowing I frowned as I spoke.

Josie tilted her head at me. "You're sure?"

I nodded. "Totally sure. I'm not saying that necessarily means anything, but it's still kind of strange."

"Well, I think we should take that as a good sign," she said, sounding a bit too cheerful. Probably, she didn't want anything to happen that had even the slightest chance of my mother and Tom backing out of the sale. Her commission on a sale like this must have been pretty hefty. "I think it means that even if we have ghosts here, they're obviously the shy, retiring type. I doubt they'll cause any trouble for your parents."

It wasn't worth the effort to point out that I really didn't see Tom as a "parent"—I'd lost the battle years before, and just went with the flow whenever someone referred to him that way.

I settled for giving a noncommittal shrug, then said, "I'm sorry I dragged you out here for nothing."

"Oh, it's no trouble." Once again, Josie tilted an inquisitive look up at me. "Are you sure you don't want to check the other rooms, though, just in case?"

I doubted that would do any good. Even in the instances where a spirit tended to haunt a particular room or single location, I'd been able to feel their presence as soon as I stepped inside a building. It should have been the same situation here.

But I figured I might as well make the attempt, if for no other reason than to make it seem as if I'd put in an effort somewhat equal to the time spent driving out here. So I said, "Sure," and made my way through the rest of the rooms on the ground floor—the enormous dining room with its table for twelve, a smaller parlor that had been fitted up as a family room, with a large TV mounted to the wall above the fireplace. That was about the only concession to modern technology I'd seen so far in the house…except for the electric lights, of course, and the shiny new-looking appliances in the kitchen.

The whole place felt quiet and serene, untroubled by any kind of wayward spirit. At the end, I circled back to the foyer and stood at the base of the staircase.

"I could go upstairs," I told Josie. "But I don't think there's any reason to do that. If any spirits are lingering here, they don't want to be seen or sensed. And if there was something dark in the house, I know I would have felt that."

Her expression relaxed. "Well, I have to say that's a relief. Although now I'm beginning to wonder whether Hank and Nora were pulling everyone's leg about the whole haunted house thing. For all I know, they liked to spread those stories because it got them some attention."

Including a segment on a cable show. Had they been playing some kind of long game, trying to stir up interest in their house in advance of putting it on the market?

I supposed that was a possibility. Since I'd never met the people in question, I couldn't begin to guess whether they were the type to pull that kind of stunt.

"Were there any reports of hauntings here before they moved in?"

"Hmm." Josie's auburn penciled brows furrowed. "I'm honestly not sure. They lived in the house for almost forty years, so anyone who would have lived here before them is gone now."

"Well, maybe there are records somewhere," I said. "Does the library have a local history section?"

The Globe library occupied a quaint brick building at the far end of downtown, but so far I hadn't visited it. No, it was a lot easier for my lazy self to just download the books I wanted from my favorite online store instead of lugging a bunch of hardbacks around.

But I was pretty sure I wouldn't be able to get any Globe history books on my phone, so maybe a trip to the library was in order…if they would even have the sort of thing I was looking for.

"Oh, yes," Josie replied immediately, relieving my fears on that score. "They have a whole shelf of books about the town and its history. That would definitely be the best place to look."

"Then I'll go see what I can find tomorrow," I said. "They're probably closed by now, and besides, I need to get out to Calvin's place after you drop me off back home."

Her expression turned almost sly. "Another date?"

"I wouldn't exactly call it a 'date,'" I said, my tone too casual. "I'm making him dinner—I just love cooking in that kitchen of his."

From the way her light blue eyes danced at that comment, I had a feeling Josie was trying to decide whether my words had a double meaning I hadn't intended.

In this particular instance, no. Calvin and I were taking things slow, and I told myself I was fine with that. He would be worth the wait.

And I really did love that Viking six-burner stove. It needed some love and attention, since he hardly ever used it himself.

"Well, it's probably a good bit bigger than your kitchen," she allowed. "The former owner did a wonderful job of renovating the flat and the store, but she still had to work with the available space."

"And it's great," I assured her. "It's just that sometimes it's nice to be able to spread out when you work."

"Then let's get back to town," she said. "I don't want to keep you."

I didn't bother to point out that Calvin wasn't expecting me until seven, and that we still had plenty of time. As far as I was concerned, my work here was done.

When I got home, I tidied up a bit and changed into one of my pretty summer dresses. As I emerged from the bedroom, Archie sent me a jaundiced look.

"Leaving again?"

Considering what a misanthrope my cursed cat could be, you'd have thought he'd be happy to have the apartment to himself for a few hours. But, even though he didn't want to come out and admit it, I sensed that Archie wasn't terribly thrilled about my developing relationship with Calvin Standingbear. Maybe he looked at it as a sort of betrayal.

Or maybe he was just thinking ahead to the inevitable moment when I spent the night at Calvin's house and didn't get home in time to give him his breakfast promptly at seven-thirty the way he liked it.

Since Calvin and I hadn't really progressed beyond some heavy make-out sessions on the couch, I had a feeling that an overnight stay was still off in the future somewhere. I didn't tell Archie that, though, mostly because I didn't think it was any of his business.

I still hadn't said anything about Archie to Calvin, either. He continued to believe Archie was a stray I'd adopted and nothing more. It wasn't so much that I felt any huge need to keep the secret any longer, only that the right moment hadn't come up so far.

Because really, it was kind of hard to find the right moment to tell your new boyfriend that your cat wasn't a cat at all, but an asexual man from the early 1950s who'd had the bad luck to attract a witch's desire, desire he couldn't possibly reciprocate, thus earning him a curse that had landed him in a feline body for the past seven decades.

"Yes," I said coolly. "But I won't be too late, since both Calvin and I have to be at work tomorrow morning. Don't throw any wild parties while I'm gone."

That remark got me a pair of slitted golden eyes, followed by the cat stalking out of the hallway and back into my office, where he usually slept.

Fine. I hadn't been put here to cater to Archie's every waking need. Still, I couldn't help feeling a little guilty as I gathered up my purse from the dining room table and headed out the door. I was coming up on the five-month anniversary of my arrival in Globe—and Archie's and my first meeting—and I still hadn't done bupkis in terms of removing that awful curse so he could go back to being a man.

Not that the delay was for a lack of trying. True, I'd been busy with running the store and seeing

Calvin on the side, but I'd dutifully ordered all sorts of arcane books from various vendors around the country, hoping that one of them would finally yield the spell I needed to get rid of the curse that ill-meaning witch had cast so many decades ago. So far, none of those books had provided the answers we needed. All I'd gotten out of the process was a shelf full of volumes I'd probably never use, since the magic I practiced wasn't generally the sort that involved itself with curses and hexes and spells that tried to warp the fabric of reality. I was just fine with doing the quiet rituals that sent out good vibes into the universe, vibes that would return to me with health, prosperity, and love.

And so far, they seemed to be working. I was definitely healthy as a horse, and the money I'd inherited a few months back from Lucien Dumond, leader of the Greater Los Angeles Necromancers' Guild, after his untimely demise at his younger brother's hands pretty much guaranteed that I'd certainly never want for anything even if my store had turned out to be a dismal failure. Which it actually wasn't, to my surprise... and probably the surprise of a good percentage of the population of Globe.

As for love, well, things seemed to be humming along pretty well in that department, too. Sure, neither Calvin nor I had said the fateful words yet, but I knew I was crazy about him, and if the warmth in his night-dark eyes as he looked at me meant anything, then he wasn't exactly indifferent, either.

I headed east away from Globe's tiny downtown and along the highway for a few miles before pulling off in San Ramon, the small settlement of the San Ramon Apache tribe. The town itself wasn't my destination, though, because Calvin's house was located several miles away, in a spot that felt like the middle of nowhere, even if it was only about five minutes or so from the highway.

That last stretch of the trip always put my poor Volkswagen Beetle to the test; the little convertible definitely hadn't been designed to bump along dirt roads that had only become progressively more rutted as monsoon season went on and we got hit by downpour after downpour on what was almost a daily basis. In fact, even though we hadn't gotten any rain that day, as I drove I noticed a few ominous flashes off to the northeast, an indication that something was brewing there.

Well, about all I could do was hope it would stay off in the distance. I really didn't relish the idea of trying to drive through the kind of blinding rain that often accompanied an Arizona thunderstorm.

Faint thunder met my ears as I got out of the car and made my way to the front door. I hadn't even raised my hand to knock before the door opened and Calvin smiled down at me. He'd changed out of his uniform and was wearing a black T-shirt, faded jeans, and scuffed cowboy boots, and definitely was the most insanely gorgeous man I'd ever seen in my life.

"Right on time," he said, and bent to give me a quick kiss in greeting. The caress was almost casual, but it still made a happy little tingle go all through me.

"It's because of my Neptune in Capricorn," I told him, doing my best to act cool, and he grinned, a glorious flash of white teeth.

"Of course it is. Come on in."

I entered the house, glad of the rush of cool air from the home's swamp cooler. That was another thing I hadn't been used to before moving here; a lot of the houses in Globe used evaporative cooling rather than air conditioning because the air was so dry, even during monsoon season, but they were surprisingly effective.

"I got everything on your list," Calvin said as he led me into the kitchen.

He'd insisted on that. It was fine for me to come over and cook for him, but he wasn't going to let me buy the supplies. I'd wanted to argue that the cost really wasn't an issue for me. However, I could tell it was a point of pride for him, and so I'd let it go.

That night, I was making London broil with a balsamic marinade, along with scalloped potatoes and salad. As he'd said, he had all the ingredients waiting for me, either set out on the polished concrete counters or sitting in the big stainless-steel refrigerator, so it didn't take too long for me to get the marinade put together and the potatoes baking in the oven.

While I was working, Calvin poured a glass of cabernet for me and set it on the counter. Once I had the initial prep done and could take a breather, I reached for the cab and took a sip. It was one we'd selected during our last wine-tasting trip to Gilbert, and I was touched that he'd thought to choose it for our wine that night.

Then, because I figured I'd better tell him the news right away and get it over with, I blurted, "My mom and her husband bought a house in Globe."

Calvin didn't look too startled by that statement, but then again, it took a lot to knock him off balance. "They did?"

I nodded and sipped some more wine. "Yes. The Bigelow mansion. You know it?"

That reply actually made him raise an eyebrow. "Everyone around here knows the Bigelow mansion. I didn't realize it was for sale, though."

"It was. Josie said there was some kind of bidding war."

Some people might have asked if my mother and Tom could afford that sort of thing, but Calvin wasn't some people. He digested my statement, then nodded and said, "It's an impressive place, from what I've heard."

"You've never been there?"

"No." He had a glass of wine of his own sitting on the counter, and he reached for it and drank some before adding, "Never had any reason to. The owners weren't the kind of people to open it up for just anyone, even though I know the historical society wanted them to give tours as fundraisers or something. I suppose Josie would know more about that."

I made a mental note to ask her when I got the chance. It didn't seem very friendly to not share such a historic home, but then again, I suppose I wouldn't have been overly thrilled at the idea of a bunch of strangers tromping through my carefully restored Victorian house.

"I'm surprised they'd sell the place at all if they were so protective of it, even if they're moving to a condo."

Calvin shrugged. "A place like that is a lot of work. And I know the current owners have been there for a really long time. They probably decided it was time to pass the baton."

And make a healthy profit on the place at the same time. Obviously, I had no idea what they'd originally paid for the place, but anyone who'd owned a house for more than forty years was going to be rolling in equity unless they'd gotten crazy about taking out second—or third —mortgages.

Since Calvin was being so mellow about the whole thing, I figured I might as well press on. "I know my mother and Tom are going to want to meet you."

Another lift of his shoulders. "Sure," he said. "Maybe we can all go out for dinner or something. I suppose it would be odd if we didn't, considering you and I have been dating for a few months now."

"You don't think it's too soon?"

He grinned and set down his wine glass, then came over and gave me a hug and a delicious cabernet-flavored kiss. "As long as they don't start asking me about my intentions, I think we'll be fine."

I smiled in return, even as I wondered what his intentions actually were. We got along very well together, that much was obvious, but neither one of us had brought up the subject of our future. For my part, I didn't want to jinx things, and I also told myself two months into a relationship was probably a bit too soon to be picking out china patterns.

If that was even still a thing.

"My mom is pretty chill, so I don't think you need to worry about that," I said. "And Tom generally follows her lead."

I didn't mention that Tom was mostly glad I'd turned out to be self-supporting despite my some-what wacky profession. His own kids were the type who always had a hand out for help; my mother hadn't said anything to me directly, but I got the impression that Tom had bought their houses and their cars for them. Great that he had the money to do so, I suppose, and yet I was proud of myself that I'd never asked for anything from my mom's husband.

"That'll be a nice change," Calvin said, some-what cryptically.

Was he referring to his own parents? He still hadn't said much about them to me, probably because he didn't want to open a line of discussion that he'd have to shut down at some point. I honestly didn't know whether they knew we were dating, although they'd have to be pretty out of the loop not to have heard *something* on the Globe grapevine.

I wouldn't ask, though. Things were going smoothly for Calvin and me, and I wanted matters to stay that way. The arrival of my mother and Tom would be a teeny little bump, nothing to worry about. And once they'd surveyed their new purchase, they'd be back off to California, and Calvin and I could continue doing, well, whatever it was we were doing.

Piece of cake.

Absolutely nothing to worry about.

That Old House Smell

THE TEXT FROM MY MOTHER CAME IN AT A little past four-thirty.

We're just passing through Mesa now. The nav says we'll be there in about an hour.

Perfect timing. I'd been a little worried that they'd show up before five, and then I'd have to decide whether to close down the shop on what was usually my busiest day of the week, but since they wouldn't be arriving until five-thirty, that gave me plenty of time to wrap things up on my regular schedule and still be out at the Bigelow mansion to greet them.

Since she'd mentioned a navigation system, I guessed that they must be driving here in Tom's fancy Porsche Cayenne SUV, and not one of his vintage sports cars. It made sense for that kind of trip, because the last thing you wanted was to have engine failure somewhere out on a lonely stretch of I-10 in the Arizona desert in early August.

I locked the doors to Once in a Blue Moon at five and stowed the cash from the register in the little safe I kept in the storeroom at the back of the shop. A quick stop in the apartment to freshen up and give Archie an early dinner—to which he shot me a baleful look but didn't say anything. I suppose even Archie knew that grousing about being fed off schedule when I was heading out to meet family members probably wasn't a good idea.

Monsoon storms had threatened all day, but now it seemed as if they planned to make good on that threat, since dark clouds had begun to bear down on the town, and thunder rumbled off in the distance as I headed out to my car. No rain yet, but I could almost smell it on the air, damp and heavy.

Well, if it was going to rain, better that it do it when I was only driving around town. I'd managed to avoid the rain when I was over at Calvin's house the other night, although sounds of thunder had troubled my sleep and I'd woken up to wet pavement and a steady drip of moisture from the eaves outside my bedroom window. At least tonight I was only heading out to the Bigelow mansion, and even though it was on the eastern edge of town, the roads were paved the entire route except for the home's driveway, which was well-maintained gravel and shouldn't be an issue.

I swung into that driveway just as my mother and Tom emerged from the detached garage, luggage in hand. Since it looked like they'd parked in the far left-hand bay, I pulled up and stopped in front of the one next to it, then got out.

As soon as she saw me, my mother dropped her suitcases and held out her arms. Like me, she was slim and blue-eyed, although her hair was dark blonde rather than the deep brown I'd inherited from my biological father. She and Tom made a good couple, because he had blue eyes and silver hair, and kept himself in shape by running and playing golf.

I'd been expecting the immediate embrace, because my mother had always been the huggy type.

Which was fine, because I was a hugger, too— if people were comfortable with it. We shared a quick, hearty embrace, and then I gave Tom a much more subdued hug.

"Everything was fine on the drive here?" I asked, and my mother nodded.

"Yes, it was smooth sailing. A little tedious— we're not used to long-distance drives—but it went well."

Thunder rumbled, and my mother looked around worriedly. "Is it going to rain?"

"It might," I replied. "It sure sounds like it wants to. We'd better get inside, just in case."

She retrieved her suitcases—I offered to take one, but she demurred—and the three of us headed toward the house. As we walked, Tom asked, "Do you get a lot of storms here?"

"Quite a few if it's a good monsoon season." I slanted a glance up at him. "Didn't you research the weather here before you bought the house?"

My mother chuckled at that question. "How would that have mattered? We'd already decided that we wanted to buy a house in Globe. I did double-check that it wasn't quite as hot here as it is in Phoenix, but that was about it."

Well, probably knowing they weren't going to bake to death in 110-degree temperatures was the most important thing. By that point, we'd mounted the steps to the porch, and Tom was pulling a set of keys out of the pocket of his khakis. Despite the lowering sky, we were nowhere near sunset, and so the stormy light was still perfectly adequate to show off all the fine details of the front door, with its stained glass and aged brass knocker.

"Oh, that's gorgeous," my mother said, leaning past her husband to get a closer look. "Photos never give you a complete impression."

"I still can't believe you bought this place sight unseen," I replied, and she only smiled.

"It wasn't 'sight unseen.' Josie Woodrow sent tons of pictures and did a video walk-through as well. But it's still not the same thing as being here."

No, it wasn't. Tom got the door open, and we all went inside, my mother *ooh*-ing and *aah*-ing over the gorgeous woodwork and all the antiques. Her husband wasn't quite as effusive, but I saw the way he eyed particular details like the carving on the mantel in the living room and the plaster medallion on the ceiling in the dining room, and I could tell he was impressed.

"Well, it seems absolutely perfect," my mother said after we'd made a circuit of the first floor. "But I suppose we should go upstairs and take a look there, too. After all, the house has seven bedrooms, so that's still a lot of ground to cover."

For some reason, a faint tremor of unease went over me. I couldn't even say why, except that maybe I was starting to second-guess myself, and I wondered if I'd made a big mistake by not checking out the second and third stories while I was here with Josie.

"Sure," I said, after noting that Tom had already nodded in agreement with my mother's suggestion. "Although I'm not sure what you're going to do with seven bedrooms. Isn't that six more than you need?"

My mother shot me an exasperated look at such a display of naïveté, but Tom replied, "Several of them are actually furnished as offices, and we both can use something like that here. The rest of them? We'll figure something out."

"We'll definitely need a couple of guest rooms," my mother put in. "Then Nick and Madison and their families will have someplace to stay if they want to come visit."

Somehow, I managed to maintain a poker face as she made that comment. While Tom's kids generally never passed up a chance to sponge off him for something or other, I really couldn't see either of them deigning to come visit poky little Globe, Arizona. They and their families all lived near the beach, and I couldn't imagine the high desert here would hold much appeal for them.

But that was Tom's problem…and my mother's as well. I wouldn't let myself worry about it too much.

"Then let's go take a look," was all I said.

The three of us headed upstairs. As advertised, the house did have seven bedrooms, along with four bathrooms on the second floor in addition to the guest bath downstairs. Everything on this level was just as beautifully furnished as the first floor, and spotless as well. I wondered if Josie had hired someone to come in and dust and vacuum while the house was vacant.

And, once again, I didn't pick up even the slightest flicker of anything that might have been a ghostly presence. No cold spots, no strange shadows, no whispery voices at the edge of my hearing.

The storm rolled in, though, bringing with it a burst of lightning, followed almost immediately by a clap of thunder.

"That was close!" my mother exclaimed.

"Probably about two miles," Tom said after a brief pause. I guessed that he'd stopped to do the mental math to figure out how many feet the sound had traveled.

"You'll get used to it," I said. "But it's been a pretty active monsoon this year. According to the locals, some summers are a lot quieter than this."

We were standing at the end of the hallway, in front of a tall window with stained-glass accents around its borders. Through it, I could see the rain pounding down, almost obscuring the trees in the garden.

Good thing I hadn't left the top down on my VW Beetle.

"That's good to hear," my mother responded. "I'd hate to think it's like this all the time."

"It's definitely not." I paused there and looked at the stairwell off to one side. "If all the bedrooms are on this floor, what's in the third story?"

Tom went over to the stairs and put his hand on the banister. It was mahogany, like all the others, but plain rather than carved. "Mostly attic space. I think there were servants' quarters up there once, but the listing said it's all just storage now."

"Let's take a look," my mother said, and headed over toward him so she could start moving up the steps.

I hung back for a moment. Something in me really didn't want to go up there. But was that actually my psychic sense kicking in, or had I just watched one too many horror movies in my formative years? The bad stuff in those films always seemed to happen in either the attic or the basement.

Since both Tom and my mother were already going full steam up the stairs, I didn't have much choice except to follow, unless I wanted to look like an idiot. Anyway, I'd already faced down Lucien Dumond's ghost when he wasn't much more than an angry wind desperately trying to tell me who'd killed him, so I told myself there probably couldn't be anything much worse in this house. After all, the previous owners had lived here for decades and hadn't reported anything worse than a cold spot here and there and a pair of eyeglasses moved to a different location from time to time.

Gritting my teeth, I fell in behind Tom and my mother. I could believe this staircase had once led to the servants' quarters, because it was so narrow that we could only go up single file.

Then my mother said, "Oh, no!" and cold washed its way down my back.

"What is it?" I asked, voice tight.

"A total mess," Tom said. "I guess we'll have to have a word with the building inspector about this."

By that point, I'd reached the top of the stairs and could see what they were talking about. Water dripped from what looked like a fairly sizable leak in the roof, pattering down on the bare floorboards.

The lump in my throat subsided. "Oh, that is pretty bad," I agreed. "Maybe there's something up here we can put under it."

Because the attic was far from empty, filled with discarded furniture and trunks and what might have been boxes of holiday ornaments. From the look of it, the previous owners hadn't taken a darn thing with them when they moved out. Clearly, they'd wanted to make a clean break.

"Good idea," my mother said. "Let's look around."

We all scattered to various corners and began

poking through the clutter. The trunks I inspected all seemed to be full of clothes that would have fetched thousands of dollars in L.A.'s vintage clothing stores, and the boxes were in fact full of Christmas decorations. Nothing there that would catch water from a leaky roof.

"What about this?" Tom asked, holding up a large flower-painted bowl.

My mother sniggered. "Do you know what that is?"

"A flower bowl?"

"A chamber pot," she said, grinning.

Tom looked like he wanted to drop the thing then and there, although a glance at the hard floor underfoot probably told him that wasn't a very good idea.

"It's okay," my mother added. "I'm sure they washed it before they stuck it up here."

"And it'll definitely catch the rain," I said.

Mouth grim, he walked over to the leak and set the chamber pot directly underneath it. At once, the drips started plinking away into the porcelain receptacle.

My mother went over as well and looked down into the pot. "It'll fill up pretty quickly at this rate."

"Don't worry," I assured her. "These monsoon storms don't last all that long. This'll hold it for now, and then tomorrow you can have someone come over and look at the roof, maybe put up a tarp until it can be repaired. Just call Josie—she'll know who to set you up with."

Tom muttered something that sounded like, "Old houses," but he got his phone out of his pocket and made the call.

While he was engaged with Josie, my mother came back over to me. "I suppose you think we're crazy for buying this place."

"No," I said at once. "It's beautiful. And you'll get the roof situation straightened out. I'll bet whoever Josie recommends will be here tomorrow, even if it is a Sunday."

Sure enough, after Tom ended the call, he said, "The workmen will be here tomorrow at ten. So I suppose that's all's well that ends well."

"Exactly," I replied. Up in the attic, the drumming of the rain on the roof had been even more obvious, but it sounded like it was beginning to slack off. "And I think our storm is moving on, so I don't think you need to worry about the chamber pot overflowing."

"There's a mental image I didn't need," my mother said, but she was still smiling.

"It's almost six," I went on. "I know it's a little early, but how about we head out to my favorite Mexican restaurant in town? My treat."

The two of them exchanged a glance. I could almost see them both wanting to protest, then realizing that buying dinner for them wouldn't put any more of a dent in my budget than it would in theirs. Besides, I was sure they'd reciprocate soon enough, probably when they took Calvin and me out for dinner. That way, they'd still be paying a bit more for our meal than I would for theirs, and they could feel good about the situation.

"Absolutely," my mother said as she looked up at Tom. "That sounds perfect, doesn't it, hon?"

He nodded, and we headed down the stairs.

My phone was buzzing on my nightstand. I blinked at the clock.

Two-forty a.m.

Who the heck would be calling at that hour?

I grabbed the phone without even looking at the screen, except to touch the green button to accept the call. When you got a call in the middle of the night, you answered it.

"Selena?"

My mother, sounding shaky and completely unlike the woman who'd laughed her way through a two-margarita dinner at Olamendi's earlier in the evening.

"What's wrong, Mom?"

A pause. "Oh, this is going to sound crazy—"

"I specialize in crazy," I assured her. "What's the matter?"

"It's…it's the house."

"'The house'?" I repeated, not sure what she was driving at. Had the roof started leaking again? But no, the monsoon storms had moved westward, and I'd gotten a nice view of a nearly full moon and a clear, starry sky just before I closed the drapes and got ready for bed.

"Yes." She hesitated, then said, all in a rush, "There were just these horrible noises that started a little while ago. Tom thought it might be the plumbing, so he went out to see what was going on. But he couldn't find anything."

"What sort of noises, Mom?" I asked, a sinking sensation starting somewhere in my midsection. Horrible noises starting between midnight and three o'clock in the morning was never a good sign.

"Like a—a banging, as if there was something inside the wall. That's why Tom thought it was the plumbing. But then it went from banging to a sort of clanging, like metal pots and pans hitting each other. Then there were the voices."

"'Voices'?" I echoed, and wished I hadn't. The word had come out a little too close to a squeak to exactly inspire confidence.

"It sounded like whispers at first," she said. "But then it turned into a horrible kind of screechy laughter. We both wondered if it might be rats squeaking, but it really didn't sound like that." A long pause, and then she went on, "Something about the whole thing just feels wrong, for lack of a better word. And normally I wouldn't bother you, but this all seems like it might be something you would know about."

The words slipped out before I could stop them. "Ready to believe in ghosts now, Mom?"

A pained little silence. "I don't know. But I've never encountered anything like this before in my life. I suppose Tom and I could leave and go to a hotel—we saw a Best Western as we came into town—but we just bought this house. I don't want to run away."

"You won't have to," I said stoutly, even as I hoped I wasn't making promises I couldn't keep. "I'll get dressed and come over. In the meantime, you and Tom stay together and wait for me downstairs. Oh, and if you have any white candles, light them all."

"'White candles'?" she repeated, sounding bewildered.

Right then I really didn't want to go into a lecture about how white candles were one of the best ways to push back against the powers of darkness. And honestly, I didn't know whether that was even what was going on here. There could still be a perfectly logical explanation for the phenomena my mother and her husband were experiencing…even if I couldn't quite think what it might be at the moment.

"Just do it, Mom. I'll be there in fifteen minutes. All you need to do is hold down the fort until I get there."

"Okay. I think I saw some white taper candles in the candelabra in the living room."

"Perfect. Light them all—and turn on every light in the house."

Another one of those long pauses. "What's going on, Selena?"

"I don't know," I said honestly. "But turning on the lights will make you feel better, if nothing else, right?"

"True. I'll see you soon."

I hung up then, and set my phone down on the nightstand. My heartbeat had sped up, and little tingles of cold worry were working their way along my spine. In my magic, I took the path of the light and did my best to ignore the darker things in the world.

That didn't mean they didn't exist.

Resolute, I went to the dresser and got out a fresh pair of jeans and a clean T-shirt.

As I got dressed, I found myself wondering if there was any place in Globe where I could get some holy water….

4

Hell's Bells

LIGHTS BLAZED FROM EVERY WINDOW AS I pulled into the driveway of the Bigelow mansion, and I found myself letting out a little sigh of relief. Obviously, my mother had taken that particular piece of advice to heart.

I got out of my Beetle, clutching the jar of moon water I'd been keeping in my fridge for the next new moon ritual. Whether it would be a viable substitute for holy water, I had no idea, but it was the closest thing I had on hand. Globe had one small Catholic church, but I doubted whether Father Estevez would have appreciated me banging on his door at three in the morning and asking for a few bottles of holy water.

As I'd driven over to the house, I'd mentally recited every spell of protection I knew, even as I asked forgiveness from the universe for doing so from behind the wheel of a car rather than properly at my altar. In my purse were packets of rock salt and coffin nails, both of which were sovereign tools for laying down protection spells at the four corners of your property.

Even so, I didn't know whether it would be enough.

I took a deep breath of cool night air—nights were almost always cool at this altitude, even during the summer— and propelled myself up the steps of the front porch. There were roughly a million other places I would rather have been at that particular moment, but I couldn't let my mother down.

And maybe if I were really lucky, this would all turn out to be bad pipes and nothing else.

No need for me to ring the bell; the front door opened as soon as I reached the top step, and my mother peered out. Tom hovered behind her, looking far more shaken than I'd ever seen him. That told me it had to be bad, since my mother's husband wasn't the sort of guy to rattle easily.

"Thank God," she said. "I think it's actually gotten worse."

Before I could respond, an unearthly clanging and banging echoed somewhere inside the house, followed by what sounded like a slamming door and a peal of shrill laughter that had roughly the same effect as fingernails dragged down a chalkboard.

All of us cringed.

Honestly, I wanted to grab both my mother and Tom by the hands and haul them back to the safe little flat above my store. After all, she who runs away lives to fight another day. But because I'd promised to come and help, turning and bolting the second I got to the property probably wasn't a very good look.

"Well," I said, doing my best to sound brisk and businesslike, even though I'd never encountered anything like this before, "let me see if I can figure out what's going on."

They stepped out of the way so I could enter the house. I'd expected to feel a chill, or the uneasy prickling at the back of my neck that was the usual sign I was in the presence of something paranormal, but I didn't sense anything.

Or rather, I didn't sense anything beyond the unholy racket that seemed to be emanating from somewhere above us, either on the stairwell or the second story.

I moved toward the stairs, even though every instinct was telling me to run. But even as my hand touched the banister and I lifted a foot to place it on the first step, the noise abruptly stopped.

My mother and Tom looked at me in bewilderment. "What did you do?" she asked.

"I didn't do anything," I said.

"But it stopped as soon as you started to go up the stairs."

"Coincidence," I offered, but she looked dubious.

Before she could say anything, though, a clock in the next room tolled the hour. Three a.m.

Three....

Rather than being reassured that the noise had stopped, I was now only more uneasy. While I hadn't made any real studies on the subject, I knew a few basic facts about demons and possession and that kind of thing.

One supposed calling card of a demonic presence—rather than your garden-variety ghost—was that they tended to be most active between midnight and 3 a.m. Why, exactly, no one knew for sure, although the theory ran that demons liked to do things in threes because it was their way of mocking the Holy Trinity. As I wasn't Catholic, I couldn't say for sure whether that particular theory was at all accurate.

"What does it mean that it stopped?" Tom asked.

"I don't know," I replied.

I was way out of my element here.

Then again, I could be jumping to conclusions. Just because the phenomena I'd briefly witnessed sure sounded like the sort of thing that went on during a demonic infestation, that didn't mean a lot. It could still be bad plumbing…a rat invasion…even a weird quirk of the house's architecture that caused strange sounds to occur when the wind was blowing from the right direction.

My mother was frowning, but then her expression cleared and she said, "Well, it seems to be gone now. How about some chamomile tea?"

The last thing I wanted was to sit down and pretend like none of this had happened. However, I'd driven all the way over here, and I supposed it would be a good idea to hang around for a bit and see if the noises started up again.

"Sure," I said, and we all trooped into the kitchen.

It was big enough that it had a nook at one end with a round table and a set of Windsor chairs. On a sunny morning, the spot was probably the perfect place to sit and drink tea and watch the wind play with the leaves on the trees and ruffle the flower petals on the garden's blooming plants. As it was, I couldn't really relax, even though all the lights were blazing and the kitchen, with its shiny stainless appliances and polished soapstone counters, looked like the last place any demon would want to infest.

My mother filled the kettle with some water,

and Tom and I sat down at the table. His expression was almost too neutral, which seemed to tell me he was busy processing what had just happened and wasn't quite ready to comment on any of it.

Fine by me. I certainly wasn't prepared to tell him and my mother that the source of the disturbance might have been demonic in nature, especially since I couldn't get any kind of psychic read on the house. That bothered me, because although I certainly didn't claim to be a ghost whisperer or anything like that, I always could tell when I entered a place that was haunted.

Maybe that particular ability didn't extend itself to demons.

As she got down a box of chamomile tea from the pantry, my mother's aura vibrated into existence for just a moment, its usual soothing sea-green now spiked with the pale orange of anxiety. I wished I could do something to relieve that anxiety, but honestly, anything I had to say would probably just make matters worse.

However, since she looked at me after she set down the box of tea, and Tom was also shooting me an expectant glance, I knew I had to say something.

Well, I'd start with the one thing I did know.

"It's strange," I said. "I'm not getting any

haunted house vibes here at all. I can usually sense ghosts, but I don't feel anything like that."

"So, what's going on?" Tom asked.

"Maybe it really is the plumbing," I told him. "Or the wind…or mice or rats."

"Rats?" my mother repeated, sounding horrified. She might have been pretty relaxed about a lot of things, but she'd always kept our apartments immaculate while I was growing up, and the house she shared with Tom always looked as though it was ready for a magazine shoot. Moon in Virgo, so it made sense.

Anyway, I had a feeling she would rather hear that her husband was cheating on her than believe her beautiful new Victorian home was infested with rats. Not that she had anything to worry about on that front; he was utterly devoted to her, and still looked at her as if he couldn't quite figure out how he'd gotten lucky enough to have such an amazing woman at his side. Then again, it sounded as if his ex-wife was a real piece of work —the kids definitely took after her—so I suppose it wasn't so odd that he'd be thrilled by being married to my mother after what he'd gone through with Sherry.

"It's just a theory," I said quickly. "But you're having the building inspector out here later this morning to look at the roof leak, right?"

Tom nodded.

"Tell him what you heard—just the facts, I mean, and not that you were thinking it might have been ghosts—and see what he has to say."

I didn't add that, since the inspector had missed the leak in the attic roof, there was the distinct possibility that he might have missed a whole lot of other things as well. This wasn't Tom's first rodeo, and I had no doubt he'd be able to approach the topic in a tactful way without sounding too accusatory.

"I will," Tom said. He rubbed the gray stubble on his chin; he and my mother were both fully dressed, in jeans and sweatshirts and tennis shoes, but their mussed hair and his stubble showed that they hadn't done anything more than that to get ready for my arrival. "I'm sure there has to be a logical explanation for all this."

"Especially since Selena can't feel anything here," my mother put in. "She's a very strong psychic."

Tom accepted that statement with equanimity. While my mother didn't talk about my powers all that much, she also hadn't tried to hide anything of who I was or what I did for a living. Now she looked proud, as if recognizing for the first time that having a psychic for a daughter might come in handy from time to time...even if she didn't really want to admit that ghosts might be real.

Unfortunately, I wasn't feeling particularly

useful at the moment. Although I didn't claim to be an authority on ghosts or anything, I'd thought I'd picked up enough information on the subject that I usually could offer some words of advice, maybe a concrete plan to address a ghostly problem. Right then, however, I felt positively flummoxed.

"That doesn't necessarily mean much," I said as the water began to boil and my mother went over to the stove to turn off the gas. "Being psychic isn't foolproof. This might be the sort of thing where you should get a second opinion."

"You mean, another psychic?" Tom asked, looking dubious.

I couldn't blame him for not wanting to drag anyone else into this. Having your new house turn out to be either haunted or infested with demons wasn't the sort of thing most people wanted to advertise.

But since it didn't seem as if my own powers were going to help me out here, we might not have much of a choice.

"Yes," I replied. My mother filled three mugs with hot water, and Tom got up from his chair to help her bring them over to the table. Once they'd both sat down—my mother nervously dunking her teabag in and out of the hot water as if it was the most important thing in the world for her to be doing right then—I continued. "I don't know anyone in the area, but I have a friend back in L.A. who has a pretty big network and can probably offer a few suggestions as to who in Arizona may be able to offer some advice. I'll call her later this morning."

All this was nothing more than the truth. I'd kept in touch with Mazey Hoskins, who ran a pagan shop in West L.A., and I knew she'd be willing to help. She did a lot of mail order stuff, and because of that, was in touch with all sorts of psychics and practitioners across the U.S. And if she didn't know someone personally she could recommend, she would still be able to reach out to some of the people in her network to see if they had any possible referrals.

Both my mother and Tom looked relieved by this suggestion. "That sounds like a great idea," she said.

"Good." Inwardly, I wondered if having another psychic weigh in would be enough to figure out what was going on, but I figured we had to start somewhere. "And in the meantime, I'm going to lay down some spells of protection on the house and the property, just to be safe."

Tom's brow furrowed slightly at the word "spells," but to my relief, he didn't protest. I suppose he figured we might as well try anything we could.

So, after drinking a bit of piping hot

chamomile tea, I ventured out into the garden, armed with a flashlight Tom gave me and the sea salt and coffin nails I'd brought from my own stash. He and my mother offered to accompany me, but this was the sort of thing I needed to do on my own. I assured them I'd be fine—even as I inwardly prayed that I actually would—and headed outside.

It wasn't quite as dark as I feared, thanks to a setting moon off to the west and, more importantly, a network of landscape lighting in the garden, subdued but definitely adequate to keep me on the paths and reveal any wild animals…or demons…that might be lurking nearby. The property wasn't anything close to a square, so I did my best to determine where the four points lay and buried the coffin nails there, along with an invocation to ensure that nothing which meant my mother or Tom any harm could venture here. Sea salt sprinkled along the perimeter of the property while I whispered more spells of protection under my breath, and then I was done.

By that point, the eastern horizon wore the faintest smudge of gray, telling me sunrise wasn't too far off. I hadn't thought I'd been outside all that long, but clearly, the night was waning, the hour inching toward six o'clock.

Good thing the store wasn't open on Sundays. I knew there was absolutely no way I could have dragged myself into work after being up half the night.

When I returned to the kitchen, it was to find my mother with her head pillowed on Tom's shoulder, eyes half-closed. She roused as soon as I came in, though, blinking the sleepiness from her eyes.

"Everything go okay?" she asked.

"I think so," I said. I didn't want to be too emphatic, just because magic wasn't what you could call an exact science. While I'd been out in the garden, I hadn't sensed anything threatening, hadn't felt as if I was in any danger. I wanted to think that was a good sign, but since I hadn't detected anything evil in the house, either, despite the horrific noises that apparently had been emanating from the stairway, I didn't know how positive I could be on the subject. Not that my instincts—good as they generally were—could be called completely reliable. They didn't often let me down, but they weren't foolproof, either.

But my mother seemed to accept my comment without reading anything else into it, because she smiled and said, "Well, that's good. I suppose we should all get some sleep now." She paused, frowning faintly. "That is, if you think it's safe."

"It feels safe," I said, and hoped I was right. "Also, the sun's coming up soon. This sort of activity tends to die down after dawn. You should be fine, but if anything else happens, just call me."

Tom put in, "I don't think it'll come to that. You need your sleep, too."

That I did. In fact, just the thought of sleep made me let loose with a jaw-cracking yawn.

My mother actually chuckled and said, "Go on home, Selena. I feel better knowing that dawn is almost here. The building inspector will be here in a few hours, and I'm sure he'll get to the bottom of it. I have a feeling we'll all be laughing about this over dinner soon enough."

That was my mother, always the optimist. I didn't argue with her, though; I wanted to believe her view of the situation was the correct one, and that I'd simply jumped to the wrong conclusion when faced with a situation I'd never encountered before.

We said our goodbyes, and I headed back out to my car and got in. As I drove away, I had to fight the feeling that I should turn right back around and stay with Tom and my mother, that something terrible was going to happen if I wasn't there.

But because I knew that was my own worry talking and not any kind of psychic flash, I kept going and hoped for the best.

"Oh, I know exactly who you should talk to," Mazey Hoskins told me over the phone. "He's even semi-local. Brant Thoreau. He lives in Sedona, but I know he'd come to Globe to check things out for you."

"Really?" I asked. It was almost eleven in the morning; I'd gone home and slept for about three hours, then gotten jarred out of sleep at nine-thirty when Archie stalked into my room and inquired in caustic tones whether I intended to feed him at all that day. Probably I should have dumped some food into his bowl when I got back to the apartment, but I'd been so tired that I'd gone straight to my room and basically face-planted in bed. I hadn't heard anything from my mother yet, and was still trying to figure out whether that was a good thing or not. I added, "Sedona is kind of a drive, isn't it?"

"I suppose so," Mazey replied. "But Brant is very keen on anything demonic."

"I'm not sure this is demonic," I said, trying to stifle a yawn. Obviously, the half a pot of mocha java I'd downed after finally rolling out of bed wasn't doing much to keep the weariness at bay. "Honestly, I'm not sure what it is."

"Well, that's why I think Brant would be perfect for the job," Mazey responded. "He has a very good sense for these things. I think he actu-ally went to seminary and was planning to be a priest, but he decided the psychic world had more to offer him."

That piece of information sounded promising. After all, if something unholy had taken up residence in my mother and Tom's gorgeous Victorian house, a lapsed seminarian was probably a better person to handle it than a garden-variety hedgewitch.

Mazey gave me Brant Thoreau's contact information, both phone number and email. I thanked her and hung up, then looked down at the notations I'd just made on the little jotter I kept on my desk.

It was a Sunday. I thought that an email might be a little less intrusive than a phone call, so I opened up my laptop and started to compose a note, wondering as I did so whether I should wait to hear from my mother as to how it had gone with the building inspector.

I'd barely typed, *Hello, Brant,* before my phone rang.

The number on the home screen was my mother's.

I immediately scooped it up. "Hi, Mom. What's the news?"

"There is no news," she replied, sounding tired and dispirited. "Or at least, nothing that Mr. Loomis was able to find. He apologized for missing the roof leak and gave us the number of a local roofer, and said he'd cover the cost of the repairs, but there doesn't seem to be anything else wrong with the house."

"I'm sorry," I said, and I was. The situation would have been so much easier if it had turned out that there really were a bunch of loose pipes banging around in the walls. Or even a rat infestation, although I knew better than to say such a thing to my mother. "But my friend Mazey gave me the contact info for someone who might be able to help. I was just about to email him."

"Oh, then, that's good news." Already she sounded much more chipper than when I'd picked up the phone. "I'll cross my fingers. In the meantime, though, Tom and I are going to go exploring. We figured it couldn't hurt to get out of the house for a bit, although it's been dead quiet all morning."

That was another piece of welcome information, even if I winced a bit at the phrase "dead quiet."

"I'll let you know how it goes with Mr. Thoreau," I told her.

"And you need to let me know when we can take you and Calvin out for dinner."

"Maybe after things have settled down a bit."

"No," she said, and although I could tell from her voice that she was probably smiling, there was a hint of steel to her tone, indicating she wasn't going to let me wriggle out of a family dinner. "I don't see any point in waiting. Give him a call and see when he's available."

"All right," I replied. "Actually, we were going to meet for lunch today at one, so I'll talk to him then."

"Perfect. Give me a call when you hear from this Mr. Thoreau."

"I will."

She hung up then, and I set down the phone and looked over at my laptop, which had shifted over to a screensaver while I was talking with my mother. I touched the keyboard, and the email I'd been about to start composing reappeared on the screen.

Trying not to sigh, I began to type.

Hello, Brant. Mazey Hoskins gave me your number. I've just encountered a very unusual situation....

5

Exit the Dragon

BRANT THOREAU'S REPLY TO ME HAD BEEN very measured, very polite, and so I had to admit I was a little startled by the apparition that showed up on the Bigelow mansion's doorstep the next day.

He was very tall, taller even than Calvin's impressive six feet and four inches. Unlike Calvin, Brant was almost painfully thin, with bleached white hair that stuck out in spikes, a nose ring, and tattoos encircling his throat and arms. A silky kimono embroidered with dragons billowed over slouchy black linen pants and a black tank top, and black flip-flops adorned feet that had black-painted toenails.

After a single blink, though, I recovered myself and extended a hand. "Hi, Brant," I said. "I'm Selena, and this is Tom and Elizabeth."

They were both staring at him, expressions owlish. Since I was used to the more flamboyant members of the psychic community and their sartorial expressions, I'd bounced back a little more quickly.

But then my mother seemed to gather herself and said, "It's very nice to meet you, Brant. Come inside."

He held up a hand, ignoring my outstretched one. "No, you need to come outside. It's imperative that I experience the house on my own, without any interference from other people's vibrations."

My mother slanted a glance at me. Clearly, she wanted me to take the lead here, since I was the one with all the experience in the psychic world.

Well, having too many people hanging around while you were trying to get an impression of a place could be difficult, so I made myself ignore Brant's high-handed manner and stepped out onto the porch. After a brief hesitation, Tom and my mother followed.

"Most of the phenomena came from—" she began, but Brant held up another hand, this one also with heavy silver rings on all the fingers.

"Don't tell me," he said. "I need to discover all this for myself."

Fine. I hadn't gone into a lot of detail in my email, only giving a brief description of the awful noises I'd heard without describing exactly where they were emanating from. It would be interesting to see if he could pick up on any of that without input from me.

"She's all yours," I said, trying to smile, and he gave me an imperious nod before he stepped over the threshold and shut the door behind him.

For a moment, the three of us stood there on the porch, staring at each other. Finally, Tom cleared his throat.

"Well, he's a personality, isn't he?"

I gave a helpless lift of my shoulders. "A lot of people in the psychic industry are kind of… quirky," I said. "But that doesn't detract from their abilities."

"If your friend recommended him, he must be very good at what he does," my mother added.

Privately, I'd been wondering just what the heck Mazey had been thinking. Most likely, she'd never met him in person, and so hadn't gotten the full Brant Thoreau experience for herself.

"Mazey is generally a very good judge of these sorts of things," I said, and left it there. After all, just because someone got my hackles up didn't mean they weren't a decent psychic.

Another of those awkward silences fell. Then I said, "Did you decide where you wanted to have dinner tonight?"

Because Calvin had been fine with the whole

"meet the parents" thing, even as he was a little surprised that they'd be interested in socializing while they had such odd developments brewing at their house. I hadn't told him about my suspicions of demonic infestation, mostly because I had absolutely no evidence to back them up. I'd only said that that the place definitely had some weird phenomena going on, and because I hadn't been able to sense any ghosts, I'd decided it would be a good idea to bring in an outside expert. We'd sort of left things there, mostly because our lunch had been interrupted by a call from one of his deputies, and Calvin had been forced to hurry off.

My mother actually smiled. "It doesn't seem as though we have a lot to choose from, based on what we saw as we were driving around town yesterday. What do you suggest?"

She was right; Globe wasn't exactly known for its fine dining. Olamendi's, the Mexican place where we'd all gone out to dinner the first night they'd come to town, was probably my favorite for dinner, but it wasn't exactly what you could call fancy. Really, there was only one obvious choice.

"Probably the restaurant at the casino," I said, even though I had a feeling Calvin wouldn't be thrilled by that suggestion. The two of us had never had dinner there, and going out to eat with my mother and Tom might feel a little like flaunting our relationship to the other members of the San Ramon Apache tribe.

Then again, Calvin was the one who'd said we didn't have anything to hide. Now he could prove it. And even if he didn't entirely approve of our dining venue, I knew he wouldn't let me down.

"Have you eaten there?" my mother asked.

"Once. It was very good," I replied, and hoped she wouldn't ask for any details. I'd had dinner with Chuck Langdon there, a dinner that had only proved we had absolutely no chemistry with each other. He'd turned out to be a good friend, and I was thrilled that things were going well for him and Hazel, but I would prefer to avoid mentioning any of that to my mother.

"A decent steak?" Tom put in, looking hopeful.

"Excellent steaks. And they have a great wine list."

Those comments seemed to convince them, because Tom pulled his phone out of his pocket. "I'll go ahead and make reservations, then," he said. "Is seven o'clock all right?"

"It's fine," I told him. "Calvin gets off at six, so I'll ask him to meet us there."

Any further conversation was curtailed by the arrival of Brant Thoreau, who threw open the front door and paused there, looking dramatic in his dragon-embroidered robes.

"Well?" I said.

His eyes narrowed slightly. In contrast to his bleached hair, they were very dark, as were his eyebrows. The contrast was startling…and purely intentional, I was sure.

"There is definitely something in this house," he replied.

My mother's hand went to her throat. "You heard it?"

"Oh, yes," Brant said. "Not as loud as what Selena described, but definitely something moving in the walls and laughing."

Even though the temperature outside hovered in the upper eighties, an icy chill crawled down my back. Those awful laughs would haunt my dreams, I was sure.

Oddly, nothing had happened the night before, on Sunday evening. My mother had told me that she and Tom hadn't slept very well, each of them tossing and turning, wondering when the next onslaught would begin, but the place had been almost eerily quiet. I'd told her that maybe my protection spells were working, but if Brant had heard something just now, that seemed to indicate the place wasn't quite as quiescent as we'd hoped.

"What is it?" Tom asked. "Ghosts?"

The single word practically vibrated with doubt. Even though he'd experienced these things for himself, it was obvious Tom still didn't quite want to admit that something supernatural might be going on here.

Brant paused. Then he said, "No, I fear it's something much worse."

"What could be worse than ghosts?" my mother said, hand still at her throat, resting on the large diamond pendant her husband had given her for their seventh wedding anniversary.

Another pause, this one even more dramatic than the first. Then, "Demons."

My mother's blue eyes, almost the same shade as mine, widened. "'Demons'?" she repeated.

"I'm afraid so," Brant replied. "I'll need to stay and gather more data, but this doesn't feel like an ordinary haunting to me."

"We already have a room set up for you," she said. "Do you need to get your bags?"

He nodded. "I'll be right back."

Because that had been part of his stipulations for investigating the Bigelow mansion—he needed to stay on the premises so he could experience the full force of the nighttime phenomena for himself. In a house with seven bedrooms, that wasn't a very big ask, and of course my mother had agreed right away.

We all watched as he walked over to a dusty white Subaru station wagon that looked far too prosaic for such a flashy individual. He got out a hard-sided rolling suitcase and a black duffel bag, and slung the bag over his shoulder and began rolling the suitcase with some difficulty across the gravel driveway.

"Do you need some help with that?" Tom asked, but Brant shook his head.

"No. This case has items I need for my investigation, and it's better if they aren't handled by anyone other than me."

One of Tom's eyebrows lifted slightly. However, he only murmured, "Sure," and stood out of the way so Brant could trundle the suitcase up the steps and into the house.

Since he hadn't told us to stay outside, we all followed him. My mother said, "You're in the bedroom on the left, closest to the stairs. The bathroom is across the hall. If there's anything you need—"

"No," he cut in. "Or rather, I won't know if I need something until I've spent at least one night here. It would be helpful if you could manage to stay out of the way."

My mother's lips compressed slightly, but her voice remained pleasant as she said, "Selena and her boyfriend and Tom and I will all be going out for dinner this evening, so that will get us out of your hair for a few hours."

"Excellent," Brant intoned, then turned away from us and proceeded to bump his suitcase up the stairs. With each step, I could see my mother wince slightly, probably as she imagined the pattern of scratches left in his wake.

Eventually, though, he reached the upstairs hall, and she let out a breath of relief. "Well," she said, sounding a little too upbeat, "I suppose that's that for now. Selena, do you want to drive with us to the restaurant, or should we all just meet there?"

"Let's meet there," I replied. "No point in you driving all the way downtown to get me. It's really out of your way."

Tom's mouth quirked slightly. "I wouldn't call a drive of less than ten minutes 'out of the way.'"

"Maybe it isn't, by California standards," I told him. "But it's not like we need to worry about parking or anything like that. The lot at the casino is huge."

"All right, then," my mother said. She gave me a quick hug. "See you tonight."

"See you tonight," I echoed, then waved at the two of them and descended the steps. I'd taken a long lunch so I could be here when Brant arrived, but I really needed to get back to the shop.

As I went, though, I had to wonder how long Tom and my mother would be willing to put up with their oddball house guest.

The afternoon passed quickly enough. Calvin texted me to confirm that he'd meet us at the casino at seven, relating that it was a quiet day and he didn't anticipate any problems with being able to get away from the station on time.

That text was a relief—not only because he'd reached out to confirm our plans, but also because he didn't seem to have any issue with having dinner at the Gold Dust. When I'd first told him about the plan, he hadn't even blinked, just nodded and said that it made sense to have dinner there, since it was definitely the nicest restaurant in the area.

So I closed up the shop, then went upstairs to change and check on Archie. He seemed to be sulking, curled up in a ball in a corner of the couch, but I knew there wasn't much I could do to improve his mood. It wasn't as though I could back out of my dinner plans just because they put my cursed cat's nose out of joint.

Clouds were building to the east once again as I walked out to my car. I'd started keeping a compact umbrella under the passenger seat ever since monsoon season had started up, so I knew I didn't have to worry even if the storm made it this way by the time we were done with dinner.

I got to the casino about five minutes early, but that turned out to be fine. Calvin was already there, chatting with the pretty girl working the hostess station. Just seeing him standing there, in jeans and a button-up shirt in a deep bricky red shade, gleaming black hair pulled back into its usual ponytail, made my heart go pitter-pat. The man looked great in his uniform, but he looked even better out of it.

"Hi, Selena," he said as soon as I walked up to him, and even bent down to give me a quick kiss on the cheek. After that brief caress, he went on, "This is my cousin Janelle. Janelle, this is Selena Marx."

"Hi, Janelle," I said, doing my best to sound casual, even though that small public display of affection had been enough to start my heart beating a little faster. Clearly, he hadn't been kidding when he said he wasn't going to try to hide things from his family.

Janelle smiled. If she had an issue with her cousin dating someone outside their tribe, she definitely didn't show it. "Nice to meet you, Selena. I'm glad you were able to convince my cousin to have dinner here. He tends to give this place a wide berth."

"Why?" I asked, looking up at him.

He gave me a lopsided smile. "Well, people come here to have fun and relax. It can be kind of awkward when a cop shows up at a casino, even if he's only there to grab a burger."

"You're not in uniform now," I pointed out.

"True," he said. "But enough people here—even the ones who aren't San Ramon Apache—know me that it can still be a little weird. It's fine, though. They'll see me here with you and your family, and will know I'm not at the casino on official business."

Almost as if mentioning my family had been an invocation, Tom and my mother came through the glass doors that separated the hostess desk and waiting area from the parking lot. Both of them looked fairly relaxed, so I hoped that meant nothing too horrible had happened at the house during the afternoon.

It was a little awkward to make introductions with Janelle looking on, but everyone was cordial —and my mother turned and gave me an approving nod as the men started to follow Janelle toward our table.

That little gesture made me feel a lot better. Of course, you'd have to be a special kind of stupid not to appreciate someone like Calvin Standingbear, but still, I hadn't known for sure how my mother would react to him. Tom had been friendly right away, although I had a feeling he was just happy that I was dating someone with a respectable job and not a woo-woo guy like Brant Thoreau.

Well, most likely Brant wasn't into dating women at all, but that wasn't any of my business.

We all sat down at the booth that had been reserved for us, and Janelle handed out menus and a wine list, then said our server would be by shortly. A few minutes were spent choosing our entrees and an appropriate bottle of wine. At that point, the waiter showed up to take our orders before telling us he'd bring out some bread and dipping oil.

It was all so utterly prosaic, I had a hard time remembering that a self-proclaimed demonologist was currently hanging out in the Bigelow mansion, waiting for another round of unearthly knocks and screams and groans to analyze. Whether that would happen while we were at dinner, I didn't know. The first attack had come in the middle of the night. Then again, last night had been utterly quiet, so maybe I just couldn't yet grasp the pattern of the phenomena.

The bread and wine arrived, and we ate and chatted, mostly about Globe and its environs. Calvin told Tom that no, there weren't any golf courses nearby, but if he didn't mind a drive of about forty-five minutes or so, he could head up to Payson and play there.

"That's an idea," Tom said. "It would get us out of Brant's hair for a while."

Calvin didn't need to ask who Brant was, since I'd filled him in on all the details during our lunch the day before. He only said, "That might be a good idea," and the conversation moved on to other topics.

All in all, I had to count it as a very successful meal. When it was over, we all walked out to the parking lot together, and Calvin and I said goodbye to my mother and Tom. After they'd gotten in Tom's Porsche SUV and driven off, Calvin turned to me.

"That went well," he said.

"Definitely," I agreed. "They really like you."

"I like them. Your mother is awesome. I can see why you turned out so well."

"Is that a fact?" I asked, my tone arch.

"Absolutely." He leaned down and brushed his lips against my cheek. "It's still early. Do you want to go back to my place for a while?"

Of course I did. Driving on the dirt road that led to his property was even less fun in the dark, but I figured that was a small price to pay for getting to spend a few more hours with Calvin.

We headed out, with me following him in his big white Durango with the San Ramon tribal police logo on the door. He'd told me after we started dating that it was his only vehicle; the tribe had decided it was better for him to drive it all the time, just in case he got called in to work at odd hours or whatever. Anyway, it had big lights mounted to a rack on the roof, and so the way out to his house was much better illuminated than it would have been if I'd been driving out there on my own.

Cool, faintly moist air met me as soon as we stepped inside. Now that we were safely alone, Calvin bent down to give me a proper kiss on the lips this time, one that tasted faintly of the flour-less chocolate cake we'd shared for dessert.

"Mmm," I said after he pulled away. "That was yummy."

"You're yummy," he replied, pushing a lock of hair away from my face. "I had a nice time."

"I'm glad." I paused there, wondering whether I should say anything else, or whether I should just let it go and allow myself to enjoy the after-glow of a friendly meal.

But I suppose something in my expression must have shifted, because the small smile Calvin had been wearing disappeared, and he said, "But you're wondering why we haven't done the same thing with my parents."

I didn't bother to protest, but instead gave a shrug. "It's okay."

"No, it really isn't." He moved away from me, heading toward the kitchen, and I followed him. Once there, he got a couple of glasses out of the cupboard, then poured us both some water. Prob-ably just as well; we'd ended up splitting two bottles of wine with dinner, and I knew I shouldn't be drinking anything else when I had to drive back to my apartment after this.

I took the glass of water from him and sipped. "The situation is totally different. My mother and Tom are regular people. Your parents...aren't. They're probably not thrilled to have their son dating a *shiksa* like me."

His brows lifted. "A what?"

"It's Yiddish for a non-Jewish woman," I explained. "I assume the San Ramon Apache have a word for people who aren't like you."

"We do." Calvin's mouth twisted slightly. "It's not exactly a compliment."

"Neither is *shiksa*," I said. "The only time I've ever heard it used in conversation was when one of my clients back in L.A. used to complain about the girls her son was dating."

That comment made him chuckle a little. "I'm sure my mother has had similar conversations with her cousins."

I couldn't really take offense at his remark. After all, we weren't talking about a difference of religion or even culture, but an entirely different race of people. I might have been a witch, but I was still an ordinary human being. It wasn't as though I could shift into a coyote whenever I felt like it.

Still....

"I do find it kind of hard to believe that in the

entire history of your people, not one of them has ever hooked up with someone outside the tribe."

Calvin looked a little pained at the phrase "hooked up," but he only said, "There might have been a few…liaisons…over the years. Nothing serious, though, nothing permanent."

How was I supposed to respond to that statement? We hadn't been dating even two months yet, so it was far too early to be thinking about anything long-term, even if I'd allowed myself to indulge in a few hazy fantasies of walking down the aisle in Globe's totally adorable Methodist church, with Calvin looking gorgeous in a suit as he waited for me at the altar. Kind of crazy, considering how long we'd been together…and not to mention the fact that back in L.A., I'd pretty much resigned myself to my single state.

Everything was different here, though, and that included my possible future with Calvin.

"They'll come around," I told him. Probably better to leave the "permanent" conversation for a much later date.

"I hope so," he said, then finally lifted his own glass of water to his lips and took a sip. "It did feel like a big step, having dinner at the casino tonight."

It was my turn to raise an eyebrow. "And there you were, acting like it wasn't a big deal."

"I didn't want to put too much pressure on the evening."

Wise of him. I drank some water as well, then said, "Do you want to go sit down in the living room?" Yes, I'd been sitting at dinner, but it felt kind of awkward to be hanging around the kitchen like this when we weren't actually in the process of making something.

"No," he replied, and set down his glass on the counter.

I stared at him in confusion. "Why not?"

"Because I can think of someplace else I'd much rather be."

After making that statement, he stepped toward me, then pulled me into his arms, kissing me deeply, making all that welcome warmth flow into my limbs. A few moments later, he pulled away...but only so he could look into my eyes.

So much passion in that dark, hungry gaze. I knew what he wanted.

Which was fine by me, because I wanted the same thing.

My fingers crept into his. "Let's go."

A phone was shrilling in my ear. I rolled over and cracked one bleary eye at the bedside table where my iPhone lay. The table didn't look familiar; it was light-hued pine, rustic and simple.

Someone in bed next to me stirred, and I pushed the last of the sleep out of my head. I was in Calvin's bedroom, in Calvin's bed. And that was him lying there just a few inches away from me, all that glorious long black hair of his spread across the white pillowcase.

Holy moly.

I wanted to drink him in—and let myself lie there and recall all the spectacular details of last night's lovemaking—but my phone wouldn't let me do that. It briefly went silent, as if it had rolled into voicemail, and then began to ring again.

"Better answer that," Calvin said, his voice husky with sleep and somehow sexier than ever.

Right. I pushed myself up to a sitting position, one hand holding the sheets and blanket and quilt against my chest so I wasn't utterly exposed. Alarm flared through me when I lifted the phone and saw that it was my mother calling.

She would never call me at seven-something in the morning unless it was an emergency.

Had there been another attack?

But they had Brant there to help them out. He was an expert in these sorts of matters…supposedly.

I touched the green button to accept the call. "Mom? What is it?"

"Selena, we need you."

Her voice sounded tight, worried, but still in control. "Um, I'm still in bed…."

Still in Calvin's bed, I thought, *with a change of clothes fifteen minutes away.*

"I know it's early," she said. "But we need you to come over. There's been an accident."

"'An accident'?" I echoed. Everything in my body seemed to clench, as if it knew in advance what she was about to say.

"Tom found Brant Thoreau's body this morning. It looks like he fell down the stairs."

6

Suspicious Minds

CHIEF LEWIS'S POLICE CRUISER WAS PARKED IN the driveway as I pulled up to the Bigelow mansion. Brant's Subaru sat off to one side, looking forlorn, as if it somehow knew its owner wouldn't be driving it anywhere ever again.

I parked close enough to the police car that I wasn't blocking the garage, but not so close that Chief Lewis wouldn't be able to get around my VW when the time came to leave. Had my mother called the police before she called me, or was it just that I'd taken way too long to get here? There was no way I could have come over still wearing my outfit from the night before, so I'd briefly told Calvin what was going on, kissed him goodbye, and then drove way too fast back to my apartment. Naturally, Archie had been waiting at the door, ready to read me the riot act for pulling a disappearing act like that, but I brushed off his complaints as I hurried into my room so I could take off my skirt and top and jam myself into a pair of jeans and a fresh T-shirt before I hurried out the door again.

As I all but ran up the front steps of the mansion, I told myself I needed to keep calm and do my best not to let Henry Lewis rile me. The two of us got along like oil and water, and the last thing I needed to do was alienate him even further.

Too bad the house was located squarely inside Globe's town limits; it would have been a lot easier—if awkward—to have Calvin handling the case, rather than Chief Lewis.

I rang the doorbell and waited. A moment later, Tom opened the door. He looked tired, but he was freshly shaven and wore a crisp pair of khakis and one of his numerous polo shirts, this one dark blue. Most likely, he and my mother had gotten up and gotten dressed before even coming down to breakfast, figuring it probably wasn't a great idea to be wandering around the place in their bathrobes when they had a house guest.

"Hi, Selena," he said, his tone subdued. "We're talking with Chief Lewis in the living room."

I followed him to the room in question, where my mother was sitting on the couch and Chief

Lewis was perched uncomfortably on the edge of the armchair that faced her. Like Tom, she was dressed and looked relatively put together, although her face was pale.

As soon as I entered the room, Chief Lewis's jaw tightened, and I saw how his aura spiked with irritated bile green before it faded out again.

Well, the feeling was mutual.

Ignoring him, I said, "Are you okay, Mom?"

"I'm fine," she replied. "I've just had a shock."

That was for sure. Between the murders of Lucien Dumond and Lilith Black, the erstwhile Instagram witch who'd descended on Globe back in June, only to be dispatched by her own assistant, I'd had enough disturbing experiences to last me a lifetime. I could only imagine what my mother must be going through right now.

She reached for the cup of coffee that sat on the table in front of her with a hand that shook slightly. Sounding just as annoyed as his aura had looked, Chief Lewis said, "Can we get on with this?"

"Of course," I said sweetly. Then I glanced over at Tom and asked, "Is there more coffee?"

"In the kitchen."

Off I went. I couldn't help glancing at the staircase as I passed by, but there was no sign of Brant's body. Obviously, the people from the medical examiner's office must have already come by and retrieved him, which meant my mother probably had waited for all that to be handled before she called me. She must have needed extra moral support, because there wasn't anything I could really add to the discussion about Brant's death. I hadn't been here when he fell down the stairs.

Maybe that was why Henry Lewis appeared extra irritated this morning. In this particular case, he couldn't possibly consider me a suspect. I'd been miles away...and I had someone who could vouch for my whereabouts the entire night. Doing so would reveal that Calvin's and my relationship had taken an important next step, but that was still miles better than being suspected of murder for the third time in less than six months.

A pot sat warming on the heating element of a fancy stainless coffeemaker. I recalled which cupboard my mother had opened to get out the mugs for our tea the night before, then got one down and poured myself some coffee. Because I'd been in such a mad rush to get over here, naturally I hadn't taken the time to get myself any coffee at home, and I desperately needed the caffeine.

Especially after my exertions of the night before. Calvin and I had slept, of course, but a good chunk of our time had been taken up by more strenuous pursuits.

Hoping I wasn't blushing too much, I returned to the living room, mug of coffee in hand.

"And you didn't know Brant Thoreau before yesterday?" Chief Lewis was asking.

My mother shook her head. "I already told you that," she said. Now she was the one who sounded irritated…not that I could blame her. Being questioned by Henry Lewis was enough to annoy anyone.

"Just double-checking, ma'am," he returned, tone and expression stoic. "And he was here because…?"

"Because he was investigating unexplained phenomena," I cut in.

"As in?"

From the way he asked the question, I could tell he wouldn't believe anything I told him, even if it was the literal truth. Well, I was going to tell him that truth, and he could just deal with it…or not.

"We weren't sure," I replied evenly. "A haunting…or possibly something worse."

His expression was frankly skeptical. "Something worse than ghosts?"

"Demons," I said.

That reply made him let out an incredulous chuckle. "You believe in demons, Ms. Marx?"

"I believe in entities that originate from planes

other than this one," I told him. "They have many different names. But I had reason to believe we were dealing with something other than ghosts."

"Brant was pretty sure it was demonic," my mother put in. She'd lifted her mug of coffee but hadn't yet drunk from it. "He heard the voices. He heard the sounds inside the wall multiple times."

"More than yesterday afternoon?" I demanded. She hadn't uttered a peep at dinner the night before about another round of disturbances.

"Yes," she said without blinking. "A little after six, and then again around midnight."

"You should have said something at dinner." I didn't want to sound accusatory, but it seemed as though she might have mentioned the demons had been at it again right before she and Tom left the house to meet Calvin and me at the casino.

She swallowed some coffee before replying, "Oh, I didn't want to bring it up at dinner. We were having such a nice time. And honestly, I was kind of glad it happened, because at least that way it didn't feel as though Brant had wasted a trip down here."

Chief Lewis crossed his arms. "Should I go wait on the porch while you ladies finish your chat?"

I sent him as sticky-sweet a smile as I could muster, but my mother immediately said, "Oh, I'm sorry, Chief Lewis. I know this must all sound pretty wild to you, but I trust my daughter's instincts. She called Brant because she knew this was outside her field of expertise. And he did confirm there was something unearthly in this house."

"Confirm how?" Henry Lewis asked, not bothering to hide the dubious note in his voice. "Did you get a signed affidavit from the demons establishing their identities?"

"Come on," Tom said, obviously not thrilled by the police chief's dismissive tone. "This is outside all our experience. And I don't know what's going on here, but it's clearly not natural."

Chief Lewis cocked a skeptical eyebrow, but he sounded measured enough as he responded, "I never heard word one about this place having *demons.* Yeah, sure, Norma and Hank liked to tell people they had a ghost—had one of those stupid cable shows about ghost-hunting filmed here—but they never turned up anything. Believe me, the people around here wear their haunted houses like a badge of honor. You should hear Norma Gallegos go on and on about the dead miner who haunts her backyard. I think she'd invite him to Christmas dinner if she could."

My mother actually smiled. "I don't think this is the same sort of thing—"

"It's not," I cut in coolly. "Demonic infestations are completely different from ordinary hauntings. We're not dealing with a human who died in this house and has lingered here ever since, unable to accept the change in their circumstance. Demons can infest a house at any time, although in general, they tend to take up residence when there's some kind of upheaval going on."

Henry Lewis's gray-frosted left brow lifted a fraction of an inch. "You seem to know a lot about demons, Ms. Marx."

"No, I really don't," I said. His opinion of me was low enough already; I didn't want him thinking I dabbled in demon-summoning or other equally unsavory activities. "At least, not anything more than someone who's done some general reading on the subject would know. But anyway, it doesn't matter that this house has a history of hauntings, because neither I nor Brant Thoreau thought it was a ghost."

At the mention of the dead man's name, Chief Lewis released a breath. "Yes, let's circle back to Mr. Thoreau. Mrs. McGill, tell me exactly what you were doing last night."

My mother glanced briefly at her husband, then set down her coffee mug and leaned against the back of the couch. "Nothing much. Tom and I went out to dinner with Selena and Calvin Standingbear at the casino. Afterward, we came home. Brant was here, listening to the walls of the stairwell with a stethoscope. The house seemed completely quiet, but he was still making notes anyway. He wouldn't tell us what he was doing, said he was still formulating an opinion. After that, Tom and I watched TV for a little while, and then we went to bed."

"Right after midnight, the noises started in again," Tom added. "They woke us up right away. We got out of bed and found Brant back in the stairwell, holding up one of those little mini-recorders so he could capture the incident."

"We have the recorder," Chief Lewis said. "It was found next to his body. I'll take a listen when I get back to the station. What happened after that?"

"The noises went on for about fifteen minutes," Tom replied. "It was nerve-wracking, obviously, but since we'd been through this several times before, we just waited it out. We went back to sleep after that."

"And Mr. Thoreau?"

"He was still in the stairwell, making notes," my mother said. "Before we went back to bed, I asked him if he needed anything—some coffee or water or whatever—but he said he was busy and that he was fine. I closed the door to our bedroom, and we went to sleep."

"You didn't hear anything after that?" the chief asked.

"Nothing," my mother replied, and Tom

nodded in agreement. "It was a little hard to fall asleep because the whole incident had put us on edge, but we managed eventually. We both slept until around six-thirty, and we took turns taking showers and getting ready, since we figured we should be put together due to having a house guest."

"What time did you finally go downstairs?"

They both looked at each other, and Tom shrugged. "I think it was a little past seven-thirty. Definitely before eight."

"We came down to get some coffee and break-fast," my mother said, picking up the story. "And that's when—when—"

"We found Brant Thoreau at the base of the stairs," Tom said, clearly cutting in so my mother wouldn't have to relate that part of the incident. "It was pretty obvious from the angle he was lying in that he'd broken his neck. That's when I called 9-1-1."

Chief Lewis nodded. For the first time, I realized he wasn't taking notes. Did he think it wasn't necessary, because this was obviously an accidental death, or was he the sort of person who filed everything away mentally and wrote it down later?

Probably the latter. He was doing his best to remain neutral, but as his aura wavered into existence again, I couldn't help noticing some orange-y spikes of suspicion.

"And you didn't hear anything?" he asked.

"Nothing," my mother said firmly. "But, like I said, the door to our bedroom was closed. Also, it's at the end of the hall, farthest away from the stairs."

A scratch of his chin, and Chief Lewis said, "Still, a grown man's body tumbling down fifteen or twenty steps makes a pretty big racket."

"Maybe so," Tom allowed, "but, like my wife said, we didn't hear a thing. Sorry we can't be of more help to you, Chief Lewis, but we really have no idea what happened."

"He must have slipped in the dark," I said. "It's tragic, but accidents like this happen all the time."

"They do," Chief Lewis drawled, then added, "But I do find it kind of strange the way tragedy seems to follow you around like a lost dog."

That was one thing Henry Lewis and I could actually agree upon. I had no idea why murder and death had decided to follow me to Globe, but three dead bodies in less than six months—especially in a town with a population of less than seven thousand people—was a bit much to blame on coincidence.

I gave a helpless lift of my shoulders.

"Well, then," Chief Lewis said, turning brisk, "I'll wait to hear from the medical examiner on the approximate time of death. Cause of death

102 • CHRISTINE POPE

seems pretty obvious, but again, I'll wait on his verdict. In the meantime, I hope you didn't have any plans to go back to California any time soon."

My mother and Tom exchanged puzzled glances tinged with worry. "Surely you don't think we're suspects, do you?" Tom asked.

"I can't say anything for sure right now," the chief replied. "It's early days to make a judgment call. All the same, I'd like you to stick around in case I have any further questions."

"We'd planned to be here for at least a week," my mother said.

"Good." He got up from the chair and brushed at the nonexistent wrinkles on his dark blue uniform pants. "I'll be in touch if I have any further questions. And definitely call me if you can think of anything else you'd like to add to your account of the crime."

"The accident," Tom told him, brow furrowing. "Brant Thoreau fell down the stairs. End of story."

For a moment, Chief Lewis didn't answer. Then his mouth lifted in a thin smile. "Fell...or was pushed. Either's equally likely at the moment." He inclined his head and added, "I'll go ahead and let myself out. You folks have a good day."

After he was gone, we all sat there for a moment, looking blankly at each other. At length,

Tom cleared his throat and said, "He doesn't actually think we had anything to do with Brant Thoreau's death, does he?"

"Deep down, no," I replied. "At least, that's what my gut is telling me. But he's not what you'd call a fan of mine, and so I think he's probably entertaining the notion for no other reason than to make some extra trouble for people who're connected to me."

My mother's mouth thinned. "That doesn't seem very fair."

"It's not," I said wearily. "But that's just the way it is. Luckily, Chief Lewis is in the minority around here. Most people are glad I opened the store, because it gives tourists a little extra incentive to stick around downtown when they're coming through."

She and Tom both nodded in a thoughtful way. I could tell from their expressions they were relieved I had allies in the town, and that I wasn't on my own when it came to dealing with Henry Lewis.

"Anyway," I went on, "why don't you come with me to see the store? It'll get you out of the house for a while, and there are some other cute little places to check out while you're down there."

The two of them exchanged a glance. "We'll do that," my mother replied. "And we also thought we'd go for a drive and get more of a feel for the area. After that…."

She stopped there, a small breath escaping her lips. Her gaze moved from the chair where I sat to the foyer, where the base of the staircase was just barely visible.

"I know it's rough," I said quietly. "But if it's any consolation, you don't need to worry about Brant sticking around the place where he died. I'm not getting any sense that he's here."

"You'd be able to tell?" Tom asked. Neither his tone nor his expression was overtly skeptical; I got the feeling he'd been exposed to enough strange goings-on by that point that he was willing to be a bit more accepting.

"Probably," I replied. "I'm not saying I'm infallible when it comes to detecting ghosts or anything like that, but I had to deal with a ghost fairly recently, and he definitely made his presence known."

And too bad that Brant hadn't stuck around. He might have been able to give me some clues as to what exactly had happened to him.

Unfortunately, it seemed as though I was going to be on my own with this one. True, Henry Lewis was investigating, but because he seemed as though he'd be all too happy to pin Brant Thoreau's murder on my mother and Tom,

I didn't think I could rely on him to do the right thing.

Both of them seemed to relax. It had to be a horrible thing to know that someone had died in your house, and so being told that person's spirit didn't seem inclined to hang around must have been a relief.

"That's good," my mother said. Once again, her gaze flickered toward the stairwell, but she didn't look nearly as tense. "I know you need to get to work, so we'll swing by a little later when we're ready."

"Sounds good," I said. "If you come by around lunch, we could all go over to Cloud Coffee. They have awesome sandwiches."

Tom brightened at that suggestion. "Sandwiches are always a good thing. So sure—we'll try to be over around noon or a little after."

With that agreed upon, I told them both goodbye and headed out to my car. The pale blue sides of my Beetle were freshly splashed with mud, as if Chief Lewis had done his best to spin some up as he maneuvered his squad car around the convertible.

I pulled in a breath, telling myself to count to three. It wasn't worth getting worked up over something so petty. Besides, I'd been meaning to take the car to the little self-wash at the edge of town for a while now. The muck would just spur me to get the errand done sooner rather than later.

As I drove away, however, I vowed to myself that I would find a way to vindicate Tom and my mother, and prove Brant Thoreau's death had been an accident and nothing more. Doing so would absolve them...and it would also annoy the living heck out of Henry Lewis.

Smiling, I reached for the button to pop the top and let the sun in. After all, it was going to be a beautiful day.

History Lesson

I'd barely unlocked the front door to the shop when Josie came hurrying in, hands already fluttering in agitation.

"Selena! I just heard!"

No point in asking her what exactly she'd just heard. News traveled fast in Globe, and Josie always managed to hear it before anyone else.

"Yes, it's kind of a mess," I responded as I went behind the display counter where the cash register was located. These days, more than ninety percent of my transactions were by credit card, but I still dutifully counted out my bills and coins and stocked the register each morning. I looked up at Josie, who'd paused in front of the counter, expression inquisitive. "Were you aware of any kind of odd supernatural activity in the Bigelow mansion?" I asked.

"Only what Hank and Nora told me," she said. "And what I already told you—a cold spot here and there, objects that would get moved around. Nothing terribly disruptive." That was pretty much the same information she'd passed along when we met at the house for the first time, but I figured it couldn't hurt to ask again. She went on, "That house has been a landmark for more than a hundred years, but there's never been any rumor that it had *demons,* for goodness' sake. Hank and Nora would've had to disclose those sorts of activities to me when they put it on the market. Besides, I was in and out of the house plenty of times and never noticed anything out of the ordinary."

Which was about what I'd thought. Of course, as I'd pointed out not even a half hour earlier, a history of hauntings didn't mean bupkis if we were dealing with demons here and not ghosts.

"What else can you tell me about the place?" I asked.

Josie pursed her lips. I could tell her mind was working away, pulling up everything she'd seen and heard about the Bigelow place. When it came to local history, the internet didn't have a thing on Josie Woodrow.

"It was built in 1897," she said. "Jack Bigelow struck it rich with his mines here, and he had the house built and brought a fancy bride from New

York who helped furnish and decorate the place, add some finishing touches, that kind of thing. They had two children, both boys. One of them moved away to San Francisco, but the other one —Sam Bigelow—stayed in Globe and raised a family here. His son died fairly young—tuberculosis, I think—but his daughter had children. The grandchildren decided to move out of state and put the house on the market. That was when Hank and Nora bought it back in the early 1970s. And they lived there for decades without a single problem. They always seemed amused by their ghost, since it was harmless."

Her story filled in some details, but the basic information was pretty much the same. The Bigelow mansion was a big, beautiful house that might have seen some tragedy over the years, and yet there was no reason to believe anything dark lurked there.

And I had to admit it was bothering me more than I wanted to admit that I hadn't been able to feel a darn thing in the place. The accounts I'd read of demonic infestations had made it pretty obvious that anyone with any kind of psychic powers—even if they were more of an empath and not a true psychic—could still sense something terribly wrong in a home that was being attacked by demonic spirits.

But here I was, falling down on the job. It

wasn't as though I'd lost all my abilities or anything, because I still saw people's auras from time to time, and I definitely was able to pick up on the vibes of other places I'd visited. No, there had to be something else going on here.

I just couldn't figure out what that might be.

"Did Sam Bigelow's son die in the house?" I asked.

"I don't think so," Josie replied, brow furrowing slightly as she dredged up another factoid from the database. "Maybe I'm remembering wrong, but I'm fairly sure they sent him to a sanatorium to treat his tuberculosis, and he passed away there."

So much for that idea.

"Do you know who else might have passed away in the mansion?"

Her mouth pursed. "I think Jack Bigelow did, but he went peacefully in his sleep at eighty-something." A pause as she sent me a questioning look. "That doesn't make him a very good candidate to be a ghost, right?"

"Right," I said. True, there were some hauntings that involved people remaining in places they'd loved and didn't want to leave behind, and not because they'd suffered a violent or painful death, but those cases were very rare.

When I didn't say anything else, Josie inquired, "How are your parents? Are they holding up okay? I feel just awful that something so terrible happened there so soon after they moved in."

"They're doing all right," I said. "I know they were a little shaken up, but really, it was just a terrible accident."

"An accident that happened because you think the house is possessed by demons."

Should I point out to her that demons possessed people and infested houses?

Probably, that fine distinction wasn't something Josie needed to worry about. "It seems the most likely explanation for the phenomena that are happening there," I said.

"I know. Al Loomis told my friend Betsy—he keeps trying to ask her out, even though she's not interested in marrying again—and she told me."

There really weren't any secrets in Globe. Good thing that Calvin and I had decided from the beginning to be open about our relationship. If we'd tried to hide it, we probably would have been doomed to failure from the get-go.

Something about the way Josie's mouth twisted she mentioned Al Loomis made my spider sense start tingling, though.

"You don't like Al?" I asked.

Josie fidgeted with the strap of her oversized purse. It was bright blue, picking up one of the colors in the blouse she wore. "I'm not one to go telling tales out of school," she said.

I planted my hands on my hips and lifted an eyebrow. That comment was just a bit disingenuous, considering she was Globe's biggest gossip.

"Oh, all right," she said, then put her purse on the counter, as if she wanted to make sure she had full use of both hands while she was talking. "I always advise my clients to work with Ted Jenkins when they need a home inspection, just because he's much more reliable. Al has slipped up too many times for my taste."

"Like the leak in the roof?"

Her mouth compressed in annoyance. "Exactly. But Hank and Nora recommended Al to your parents, and so they decided to work with him. I think they were just trying to have the process go as smoothly as possible, but it bothers me because I can't help but think there may be other issues with the house he may have missed."

That sounded like my mother and Tom. Both of them were all about not making waves, so I could see why they would have gone with the owners' recommendation for the home inspection.

"Well, let's hope not," I said lightly. "Still, it's not Al's fault that something supernatural may be going on with the house."

Josie didn't reply right away. From the glint in her light blue eyes, I got the impression that she'd be all too happy to blame him for everything she could. "Maybe," she said at last, reluctance clear in her voice.

"Besides," I went on, "Tom's business is plumbing supplies, and if he says a noise couldn't possibly be a plumbing issue, then it's best to listen to him. Whatever's happening in the Bigelow mansion, it's something much bigger than a minor mechanical issue that Al Loomis might have overlooked."

"I suppose so." She paused there, then said, "It's just awful that that man from Sedona died in the house, though. Does Chief Lewis have any theories?"

"Not really. He's waiting for the medical examiner's official report."

She nodded. "Well, it sounds like a terrible accident and nothing more. Those stairs are quite steep—the house was built before that sort of thing was standardized, of course. I was glad I didn't have to show the place too many times before your parents expressed interest, just because the steps aren't much fun for someone short like me."

I hadn't noticed, but then, at five foot eight, I had a good six inches on Josie Woodrow.

Her phone buzzed, and she reached into her cobalt-blue purse and drew out her iPhone in its sparkly red case. A frown creased her brows, and she said, "Oh, dear. One of my clients is having issues with the title company, and I have to jump in and save the day." She returned the phone to her purse, then reached across the counter to give my hand a reassuring pat. "You take care, Selena. And let your parents know that I'm here for them if they want to have any additional inspections performed on the house."

"I will," I replied. Awful as the situation was, it always felt good to know that I had Josie in my corner. She was probably the most capable person I'd ever met. "Thanks so much, Josie."

After she sailed out, I went into the stockroom and got out a few more packs of Tarot cards to add to the display. For some reason, there had been a real run on them the week before; I got the impression that Tarot was the latest fad among some of the local high school girls. It seemed odd to me that schools were already back in session in Arizona when it wasn't even the middle of August yet, but they did things differently here from what I was used to back in California.

A few customers came and went, and then a little after twelve, my mother and Tom walked in. Judging by the way they gazed up at the mural my friend Hazel had painted on the ceiling, and looked around at the displays of books and crystals and clothing, they were duly impressed. I couldn't quite help feeling relieved; it wasn't that I needed my mother's approval or anything, but it still felt good.

"Why, Selena, it's beautiful!" she exclaimed.

"I sent you pictures," I returned, and she shrugged.

"Oh, that's not the same. It's so much better to be able to experience the store in person."

"It is very nice," Tom agreed. "For some reason, I didn't think it would be this big."

Even though he was too polite to say it, I got the impression that he'd thought my store must have been some hole in the wall, despite the pictures I'd sent my mother. "Well," I said diplomatically, "it's about the same size as my apartment, and so that means it's just a little over seventeen hundred square feet."

He nodded, and wandered off to inspect one of the bookcases. My mother came closer to the counter so she could look at the jewelry and crystals locked away under the glass.

"Are you okay?" I asked in a low voice.

That question got me one of her sparkly, too-bright smiles. "Oh, we're both fine," she said. "I'm not saying it doesn't feel good to get out of there for a bit, but Tom and I have both agreed that we need to put this behind us. It's really a beautiful house, and I'm sure we'll get the whole thing sorted out eventually."

Demonic infestations weren't always the kind

of thing you could "sort out," but I didn't want to argue with her.

"How was the house after I left?" I asked instead.

"Quiet," she said at once. "We waited to leave until a little after twelve, just because we wanted to see if there was going to be a repeat of the disturbance we had at noon yesterday, but nothing happened. It felt…peaceful."

That reply made me frown slightly. Was it possible that the infestation was over, that, once the demons had managed to get someone killed on the premises, they'd decided their work was done and had moved on to the next place?

No, it couldn't that easy. Then again, we were talking about demons here. It wasn't as if they had to function by normal rules of human logic.

"That's great news," I said. "Are you two hungry? I can close up for a bit, and we can walk over to Cloud Coffee."

"Yes, we're starving," my mother said, now looking a bit more chipper. "We never ate any breakfast because of…well, what happened."

"Then you definitely need one of Kris's world-famous Monte Cristos."

That suggestion only made her shake her head. "Oh, I think that's way too many calories for me. I'm sure there must be something else that would be a bit healthier."

Considering that my mother had managed to hang on to her size-six figure into her fifties, I thought her worry was a little misplaced. I wouldn't argue with her, though. I only said they had a great chicken salad wrap, too, and after that we scooped up Tom and headed out.

The day was sunny and bright, the air warm but not uncomfortably hot, extremely pleasant for August. It was hard to believe that someone had died earlier that morning in the house Tom and my mother had bought. But no matter how cheerful Globe's downtown looked right then, I knew the mystery of Brant Thoreau's death would continue to hang over us.

Well, until someone managed to figure it out.

Cloud Coffee was crowded, so we ordered our sandwiches to go and brought them back to my apartment. As soon as the three of us entered the place, Archie bolted back to his refuge in the office.

"I didn't know you had a cat," my mother said.

No, I'd purposely avoided mentioning Archie, mostly because I didn't want to make the mistake of saying too much about him. "Oh, Archie?" I said, trying to sound innocent. "He was a stray I took in. I found him wandering around the first day I was here, and we just sort of adopted each other."

That story was close enough to the truth. She definitely didn't need to know he wasn't really a cat at all.

"It's nice when you own your place and don't have to worry about landlords telling you whether or not you can have pets," my mother responded. No doubt she was remembering the years after we lost my one and only pet, Star Ruby, and how I'd begged to get another cat after we'd moved and I learned the hard way about apartments and pet policies. The first place we'd lived had been pretty lenient about such things, but the ones that followed were much stricter.

"Definitely," I agreed.

We talked about cats—although she and Tom currently had a dog, Winston, a fluffy little Maltese who was being watched by a pet sitter while they were out of town—and soon enough, one o'clock rolled around and I needed to get back down to the shop. Or rather, I felt I needed to get back to work. I kind of doubted anyone was beating down the door to get into Once in a Blue Moon.

My mother and Tom said goodbye, and told me that maybe we could get together for dinner again the next night. I offered to cook dinner, and my mother tried to beg off.

"Oh, I don't want to put you to all that work," she protested.

"I like to cook," I said. "And there's plenty of room for all of us in the dining room here. I'll see if Calvin can come over."

"That would be nice," she replied. "But I don't want you to think that you and Calvin always have to double-date with Tom and me."

"I don't," I told her, my tone firm so she'd know I was only telling her the truth. "Anyway, the only time Calvin gets home-cooked food is if I make it—or his mother sends him a care package —so I'm sure he'll be down with it."

Those words made her smile. "All right."

She gave me a quick hug, and I walked her and Tom down the stairs. From there, they headed out to the parking lot, and I went into the shop.

It seemed my belief that no one would be waiting for me to return from lunch had been a misplaced one. A woman around my age, maybe a little younger, was peering in one of the display windows, all but pressing her nose to the glass. She had long, honey-blonde hair that fell in fluffy waves nearly to her waist, and a pretty face with a pointed chin and straight little nose, and wore a tie-dyed skirt and turquoise blue tank top.

In short, she looked exactly like the sort of person who'd be jonesing to get into a New Age shop.

"Sorry," I said as soon as I unlocked the front

door and opened it. "I got a little delayed coming back from lunch."

Up close, her eyes looked reddened, as if she'd been crying fairly recently. "Are you Selena Marx?" she asked.

"Yes," I replied, somewhat uncertainly. True, my name was on the Yelp page for the shop, and probably wasn't too hard to Google, but this was the first time I'd had someone come in the store and ask for me directly by name.

"I'm Sasha Young," she said. "Brant Thoreau was my boyfriend."

"Oh, I'm so sorry," I said, even as I thought, *So much for my women's intuition about his sexual orientation.* "Please, come in."

She followed me into the shop and paused by the rack that held a collection of embroidered and sequined skirts from India. Looking diffident, she said, "The police told me he died at your parents' house. I tried to go by and talk to them, but no one was home."

"They went out for the afternoon," I told her. "It was hard for them to be there, so they decided to get out for a bit."

Sasha nodded, red-rimmed blue eyes sympathetic. "I can understand that. Do you know what happened? The police wouldn't tell me much, except that he fell."

"That's about all any of us know," I said. "He

came to the house to investigate a possible demonic infestation, but he fell down the stairs in the dark."

"Fell…or was pushed," she responded, echoing Chief Lewis's words from that morning. However, her implication was entirely different. "Demons can do that, you know."

"Push people?" I asked. Hopefully, that question hadn't sounded too skeptical.

"Yes. But Brant was careful. I don't see how they could have gotten the better of him like that."

I didn't, either. However, the thought of demons causing evil mischief such as physically shoving Brant down the stairs made the hairs stand up on the back of my neck, so I pushed it aside as best I could and said, "I really think it was just a terrible accident. What else did the police tell you?"

"Not much."

Sasha let out a sigh, looking even more pale and tragic, and I said, "Do you want to sit down? There's a chair over by the dressing room."

Because I did have one tiny little cupboard where my customers could try on clothes, along with a seat in case they had any bored husbands or significant others with them while shopping.

"No, thank you," she said. "I'm too on edge to sit down. I have to wait for the medical examiner to release Brant to a local funeral home, and after that I'll be able to take him back with me to Sedona."

"'To Sedona'?" I repeated, not sure what she was implying.

"To scatter his ashes," she said. Her expression shifted, and she glanced up at me with a vaguely impatient look in her eyes, as if it should have been patently obvious what she'd meant. "We have a friend who's a drone pilot, and he's going to scatter Brant's ashes over the Secret Mountain Wilderness area outside Sedona."

That actually did sound kind of nice… although I had to hope no one would be hiking in the area when Brant was released to the four winds, so to speak.

"Won't that all take some time, though?" I asked. Not that I pretended to be an expert on the matter, but I knew when Lucien was killed, it had been several days before his body was released to his family. The same thing with Lilith Black, except it had been her business manager and assistant who'd had to take on the grim task of bringing her body back to Los Angeles.

"A couple of days, probably," Sasha said. "I booked a room at the Best Western. I figured in the meantime, I'd see if I could get any more information about what really happened to Brant."

While I completely understood her motivations, I figured I should probably give her a piece of friendly advice. "Chief Lewis doesn't much appreciate civilians interfering with his investigations," I told her. "I know this from personal experience."

"Because you're the one who really solved the murders of Lucien Dumond and Lilith Black," Sasha replied, and I blinked at her in astonishment. Before I could start to respond, though, she continued. "I know all about that stuff. Those stories were all over my Facebook groups and witch forums. You're kind of a celebrity."

"Oh, I don't think—" I began, but she waved me off.

"No, it's true. Selena Marx, hedgewitch detective. It's pretty cool." She stopped there before adding, "That's another reason why I wanted to talk to you. I know Brant's death had to hit close to home for you because it happened in your parents' house, but I realized as I was driving down here that you were the perfect person to help me out." Another pause, and then she said, "I want to hire you to find out who really killed Brant."

8

Hedgewitch Detective

FOR A SECOND OR TWO, I COULD ONLY boggle at Sasha's suggestion. Then I managed to gather myself and said, "I'm not a detective. I just had a little luck piecing the evidence together in those two murders. And really, in the case of Lilith Black, the killer basically confessed the whole crime to me, so it wasn't as though I had to do any kind of real work to figure out who was guilty."

This demurral didn't seem to have much effect on Sasha Young. She crossed her arms and stared at me directly as she said, "Well, I can't rely on Chief Lewis. He's just another authoritarian with a buzz cut. He doesn't even want to entertain the possibility that there might be a supernatural element to all this."

Since I couldn't really argue with her assessment of Henry Lewis, I figured I'd better try another tack. "None of us knows for sure if that's actually the truth. The house feels really blank to me, for lack of a better word." I paused after making that comment, because Sasha was still standing there and staring at me with an expectant expression on her face, like a kid who's opened all her birthday presents but thinks there must be one or two stashed in a closet somewhere. "And you don't have to hire me," I added. "I want to find out what happened just as much as you do."

Her expression was dubious but at the same time almost relieved. I had a feeling she really didn't have the money to spend on a private detective, witchy or otherwise. "Are you sure?" she asked.

"Positive," I replied. A sudden notion struck me, and I said, "Are you psychic, Sasha?"

"No," she said, looking a bit downcast. "I'm an empath and a Reiki practitioner, but I don't get vibes from places unless they're *really* full of bad juju, like a house where someone's been abused for years. Things like that."

I knew exactly what she was talking about. Several times in my life, I'd been in places thick with a miasma of anger and resentment and pain, places that felt as though they were choked with cigarette smoke even though the air was clear to the naked eye. Being in a haunted house was entirely different, though. It was more like I could sense something at the edge of my hearing and my sight, something I instinctively knew was there even if I couldn't see it for myself.

"Well," I said, "I just don't get anything when I walk into the Bigelow mansion. Not even—not even after Brant died there."

"He's moved on, though, right?" Sasha asked, her pretty, pointed face now tight with anxiety.

"As far as I can tell. I don't feel him there, that's for sure."

For a second or two, she was silent, letting herself come to terms with that information. Maybe she would have preferred him to be a ghost, since at least that way, she could still have some kind of contact with him. Then a certain light came into her blue eyes, and she said, "You didn't know Brant, right?"

"No, I didn't," I replied. "I met him very briefly when he came to the house to check it out, but I didn't stick around because I had to come in to work."

"Well," she said, "isn't it possible that you couldn't sense him because you didn't know him at all? Maybe I should go to the house and take a look."

That didn't sound like a very good idea. I could try to convince myself I was only being cautious, but honestly, I just didn't feel like setting foot in that house any time soon. "I don't know —" I began, and Sasha shook her head.

"It's worth a try, isn't it?"

"I don't have a key, and no one's home," I pointed out.

"You can call your parents and see if they have a spare. Or maybe the realtor who sold them the house still has one, since they bought it so recently."

That was probably the easiest solution. If anyone still had a key, it was Josie. However, I didn't think it would be kosher to pick up a key and go barging in there without permission from Tom and my mother.

"Let me call my mom first," I said.

Sasha seemed content with that; she leaned against the counter while I got out my phone and made a quick call. To my relief, it went through at once. Service in and around Globe wasn't always the most reliable thing in the world, and it was entirely possible that the two of them could have been out driving around in a cellular dead zone.

"Selena!" my mother said, sounding surprised. "Is everything okay?"

Depends on your definition of "okay," I thought, but I only said, "Brant's girlfriend is here. She wants to take a look at the house. Is that okay?"

"Brant had a girlfriend?" my mother asked,

her tone even more startled at that particular revelation.

I held back a grimace. "Yes. She'd really like to go to the house and take a look around, but I thought I'd better check with you first."

"It's fine." Her voice sounded full of questions, but apparently she realized it would be better to ask later, because she went on, "There's a spare key under the stone frog by the front porch. And actually, it's good that Brant's girlfriend is here—the police took his mini recorder and stethoscope and phone, but they left behind his bags. Tom and I were wondering what we should do with them."

Right. I'd completely forgotten about the overnight bag and the suitcase Brant had brought with him. It had seemed a lot for a quick trip, but maybe he'd over-packed because he didn't know for sure how long the investigation would take.

"Okay," I said. "We'll make sure to get them. Thanks, Mom."

"Oh, it's fine." Just the slightest pause, and then my mother added, "Please tell her we're sincerely sorry about what happened."

"I will."

I ended the call to see Sasha watching me expectantly. "We can go on over," I told her. "There's a spare key hidden by the porch."

Some of the tension in her face eased. "Oh, good."

"And you can get Brant's bags. They're still in one of the guest rooms."

All she did was nod, but I could tell she was glad that she'd be able to retrieve some of his belongings, even if the Globe P.D. was hanging on to those items they thought were most relevant to the investigation. I hoped they'd release them at the same time they sent his body to the funeral home, but I supposed that was up to Chief Lewis.

I asked Sasha if she wanted to drive with me or follow me to the house, and she said, "I'd better drive with you. Brant's car is still there, isn't it?"

Right. The police had left the Subaru sitting in the driveway, probably because it didn't have anything directly to do with the investigation. It wasn't blocking the bay where Tom had been parking his Porsche Cayenne, so it had probably escaped his mind that they'd have to do something about it eventually.

"It is," I said. "But won't that leave you with two cars here in town?"

Her thin shoulders lifted. "It will, but I'll just leave Brant's car in the hotel parking lot until I can come back with a friend to drive it to Sedona. That would be a lot cheaper than having it towed a couple of hundred miles."

That was for sure. Sasha seemed a little steadier now, maybe because we were discussing logistics, something concrete and manageable to focus on.

"My car's out back," I went on. "We might as well head out."

I locked the shop door and returned my much-used "be back at" sign to the front window, and the two of us went through the back door and out to the parking lot. The day had heated up, although thunderheads were building to the east, and I had a feeling we'd have another round of monsoon storms later that afternoon and possibly into the evening.

Right then, I couldn't think of anything I wanted more than to go back to Calvin's house and sit in his comfortable living room, snuggled together on his beat-up leather couch while the rain pounded down outside and we shared a bottle of wine. I'd sent him a couple of texts to let him know what was going on, but he hadn't been able to do much more than respond with brief, sympathetic replies. It sounded as though he was caught up in his own troubles on the reservation. Not a murder, thankfully, but the discovery that some squatters had decided to set up a meth lab in an abandoned house near the eastern edge of the San Ramon tribe's territory. He'd said he'd try to make dinner the following night, but a lot depended on whether the squatters were acting alone or whether they were part of a bigger supply chain that would require further investigation.

I held back a sigh, and told myself that missing an evening with Calvin wasn't the end of the world. I still had him, and I wasn't grieving the loss of the man I'd loved, unlike the woman in the passenger seat of my Beetle.

She didn't say anything on the drive out to the Bigelow mansion, only watched the buildings and streets pass by as we left downtown and headed up Globe's hilly roads to our destination. As we pulled onto the long lane that wound its way toward the house, however, she let out a brief sound of surprise.

"What is it?" I asked, allowing myself a quick glance over at her.

"I don't know," she said. "I suppose I didn't expect it to be so beautiful."

It was a stunning house, that was for sure. I had to hope that one day it could be appreciated again for its architectural beauty and not because of what had happened inside.

After we parked, Sasha allowed herself one melancholy glance at Brant's Subaru, getting dustier by the day as it sat in the driveway. But then she marched up the front walk, clearly intent on getting inside as quickly as possible.

I had to pause to retrieve the spare door key from its hiding place under the stone frog, but soon enough we were inside. Despite the warmth of the day, it felt almost cold as we walked into the foyer. Of course, no supernatural cause there; I saw that the thermostat near the door had been set to a chilly sixty-five degrees. My mother, probably; thanks to her ongoing hot flashes, she was always complaining that it was too warm and tended to crank the A/C wherever she went.

"It happened there, didn't it?" Sasha asked with a significant glance toward the stairwell.

Since it seemed as though Chief Lewis must have filled her in on some of the details of Brant's death, I didn't see any reason to deny it. "Yes," I said simply. "We all think he must have slipped in the dark. He was wearing flip-flops."

That comment almost made her smile. "He always wore those, except in the dead of winter. I used to tease him about tripping over things, but…."

Her words trailed off, and she released a breath.

Hoping to ease the tense moment just a little, I said, "Do you want to go upstairs and get his stuff?"

"I guess I'd better."

Although Sasha hesitated for just a second before she put her foot on the bottom step, after that she seemed to find her stride, because she moved quickly and confidently up the stairs. I followed, glad that she obviously was tougher than she looked.

When she got to the landing, though, she paused, waiting for me to join her. "It's the room just across the hall," I said, and headed over to the door, which stood open.

The quilt looked slightly rumpled, as though Brant might have sat down on the bed at some point, but it definitely hadn't been slept in. His overnight bag rested on the wing chair in the corner, and his suitcase had been left in the closet, which was otherwise empty. Obviously, he hadn't bothered to unpack. Why, I didn't know, since hours had passed between the time he arrived at the house and the time he made that fateful decision to investigate the noises on the stairwell.

Without speaking, Sasha went to the chair and picked up his overnight bag, while I rolled the suitcase out of the closet.

"He didn't unpack," she said.

"No," I agreed, since that much was obvious.

"I wonder why?"

Since I could only guess at his motivations, I shrugged. "Maybe he was waiting to see if there was anything worth investigating."

"Maybe."

She sounded dubious, though, as if she wasn't quite sure that was the reason why he hadn't tried to settle in a bit. For a moment, she stood in the middle of the room, both hands wrapped around the handles of the canvas bag she held. Then she said, "I think you're right."

I tilted my head at her. "Right about what?"

"About this house." Her gaze traveled the room, which was just as carefully furnished as the rest of the Bigelow mansion—the walls had wallpaper striped in dark green and cream, and the quilt and curtains echoed that color scheme. A rug in muted tones of green and beige covered the polished wood floor. Bright afternoon sunlight streamed in, illuminating a few dust motes that danced like tiny fireflies.

Before I could respond, she continued.

"It feels...good. Like happy people lived here. I know I don't have your sense for these sorts of things, but still, I think I would be able to tell if it was evil. And it's not."

Exactly my sense about the whole thing. Unfortunately, I didn't know whether the house felt that way because I desperately wanted it to, or whether I'd been completely off-base about the whole demon thing, even if there hadn't seemed to be any other halfway plausible explanation for the disruptions my mother and Tom had experienced and which I'd heard for myself.

"The demons could be gone," I said, although that didn't feel quite right, either. Once again, I felt as though I was missing something vital about the situation, even if I couldn't put my finger on what it might be. "Or maybe something else is going on. But my mother and her husband both wanted to tell you how sorry they are that this happened."

Sasha nodded, but then her purse started playing "We Are Starlight," and she gave me an apologetic look and set down the overnight bag she was holding so she could pull out her phone. "I think it's someone from the police station," she said as she glanced down at the screen. Then she held the phone to her ear. "This is Sasha Young."

A long pause, during which she appeared to be listening intently to the person on the other end of the line. About all I could do was stand there. I suppose I could have taken the suitcase and headed back downstairs, but my instincts were telling me I needed to stay with her. Whether that was because it just seemed safer to stick together, or because I really wanted to know the reason for the call, I couldn't say for sure.

Then she said, "Thank you, Chief Lewis. I can be there in about twenty minutes," and ended the call before slipping the phone back into her purse. She met my inquiring gaze and added, "They're sending Brant over to the funeral home now, and they're releasing his personal effects. I need to go by and pick them up."

Her voice was steady enough, but I could see

tears gleaming in her eyes. Gently, I asked, "Do you want me to come with you?"

As soon as the words left my mouth, though, I found myself wondering if that was such a great idea after all. I kind of doubted that Henry Lewis would be jumping for joy once he found out I was helping Sasha. If he could have coerced the city council into writing an ordinance that banned me from amateur investigations, he probably would have been all over it.

But it was too late to take back the offer, because Sasha said in tremulous tones, "Oh, would you?"

"Of course," I said. "I wouldn't have offered otherwise."

That settled, we headed downstairs, bringing Brant's luggage with us. As we went down the stairs, I found myself stiffening, as if expecting the unholy racket my parents had reported to start up as soon as Sasha and I passed by the landing, but everything remained silent.

Maybe the demons really had decamped once their unholy work was done.

We took the suitcase and overnight bag to the Subaru and stowed them in the back. "The police station is only a couple of blocks away from the store," I told her. "You can follow me to the parking lot."

"Sounds good."

I got in my car and maneuvered it around so it was pointing in the right direction, then waited while Sasha did the same. From there, we headed back downtown, passing my store as we went. I noticed someone peering in the window, their dejected stance telling me they weren't happy about the shop being closed.

No point in worrying about it. If they really wanted to buy something, they would come back. Still, I was glad I didn't have to rely on the income from the store to maintain my lifestyle.

The parking lot at the police station only had a handful of cars in it. Not surprising; Globe wasn't exactly what you could call a hotbed of criminal activity. I got out of my Beetle and went to meet Sasha, who surprised me by saying, "I'm glad you came with me, Selena, but maybe you should wait outside. You're not exactly besties with Chief Lewis, right?"

I couldn't help smiling. "There's an understatement."

"Then I'll just go in and get Brant's stuff and come right back out." She hesitated, then added, "But I'd really like it if you could come with me to the funeral home. Chief Lewis said I needed to go over there to make the final arrangements."

"Whatever you need," I assured her. Although I knew none of this was my parents' fault—or mine, despite my feelings of lingering guilt over calling in Brant for a consult—I felt as though I needed to do what I could to help Sasha out.

She nodded and headed off toward the entrance to the station. I lingered by my car, praying that Henry Lewis was inside working and wouldn't choose that moment to pull up to the station and spot me lurking there.

Off in the distance, thunder rumbled. It sounded as though the storms today were going to make an appearance sooner rather than later, and I hoped we'd be able to get our business handled before the rain showed up in Globe. I'd come to love monsoon season, but it was definitely better enjoyed from inside the comfort of your own home or business, rather than hanging around in a parking lot.

To my relief, Sasha emerged from the station only a few minutes later, carrying what looked like a brown paper shopping bag. "Brant's stuff," she explained briefly. Then she reached into the bag and handed over a small voice recorder. "I thought you might want to listen to what's on this."

"Don't you?" I asked.

She shook her head. "He was holding it when —when it happened. It might have recorded his fall. I don't want to hear that."

Ouch. I couldn't blame her for feeling that way. I didn't really want to listen to it, either, but I knew I needed to, just in case there was something

I could pick up that no one at the police station had caught. They probably had analyzed the recording to see if they could detect any sounds of human foul play; I'd be looking for something entirely different.

"Sure," I said. "I'll listen to it after I close up the shop. If I hear anything that might provide a clue, I'll let you know."

My words obviously were a relief, because she sagged a little. "Thanks, Selena."

"It's the least I can do." I hesitated, but I knew I had to ask. "Do we need to go to the funeral home now?"

"Yes," she replied. "The deputy told me it's over on Hill Street."

"That's only a couple of blocks away," I told her. "You can follow me again."

With those arrangements made, we both got in our cars and drove to White Funeral Home, Globe's one and only mortuary. It was a brick building with white shutters and columns, vaguely Southern colonial in appearance, and sort of out of place among the town's Victorian and Craftsman architecture.

The rep who greeted us was a cheerful-looking woman in her late fifties, with a friendly round face and ginger hair piled high on her head. "I'm so sorry for your loss, Miss Young," she said as she ushered Sasha and me into her office. Clearly, someone at the police station—maybe the same deputy who'd handed over Brant's effects—had called to let the people at the funeral home know we were coming. "I'm Janice Hollowell. Please take a seat."

We both sat in front of Janice's big mahogany desk. The place was decorated in what I thought must be typical funeral home style—dark wood furniture, heavy faux satin curtains at the window, subdued tones of cream and wine and deep blue.

"I want Brant to be cremated," Sasha blurted out, as if she needed to get that part of the process over with as quickly as possible.

Janice sent her a friendly smile. "Of course. You'll need to choose an urn."

And she pushed a binder full of photographs across the desk.

Sasha took it and leafed past a couple of pages, then bit her lip. "These are all really expensive," she murmured, clearly dismayed.

"Don't worry about that," I said quickly. "Choose whichever one you want. I'll take care of it for you."

"You don't need to do that," she protested. She'd paled again, but I could tell she was doing her best to keep it together. "Besides, we're going to be scattering his ashes. It's not like they're going to be sitting on my shelf."

"Still," I said. "Aren't you going to have a service for Brant before you do that?"

She seemed to consider my question for a moment. Sounding hesitant, she said, "I—I guess I hadn't really thought about it. But I suppose his friends will want something."

"Then go ahead and pick the one you think he would've liked best."

A nod, and then she started leafing through the binder as Janice gave me an approving look. Clearly, she wouldn't have been happy if she'd had to hand over Brant in a plastic box.

After flipping through the entire binder, Sasha went back a few pages and left it lying open so I could see the page in question for myself. "I think he would've wanted this one."

It was beautiful—a tall vase shape of fired pottery and a "tree of life" design done in bas relief, the whole thing finished with a reactive glaze in warm shades of green and brown. Honestly, I would've chosen it to hold pussy-willow branches on my mantel if I hadn't known what its actual intended purpose was.

And it wasn't cheap, but I didn't care about that. I took my credit card out of my purse and handed it over to Janice, while Sasha looked on with guilty eyes. After the funeral director left the room to process the payment and make the other arrangements, Sasha turned to me.

"I really didn't expect you to pay for all of this."

"It's no problem," I said. "I want to help. I feel like it's partly my fault that this happened to Brant. If I hadn't called him to help us out—"

"You shouldn't think that," Sasha cut in. "Brant was very excited about this case. He hadn't been called on one for a while, and he thought he would be able to make a difference. But still... thank you. I was wondering how I was going to afford all this."

It had been a while since I'd had to worry about expenses from week to week, whether I'd be doing enough readings to make rent and pay the utility bills, but I still remembered what that was like. Just one car repair or trip to urgent care was enough to make a person wonder if they'd be able to cover their basic expenses that month. And paying to cremate someone and buy an urn was not cheap.

"Well, now you don't have to," I said, trying to sound reassuring. I paused, then asked, "What are you going to do after this?"

"Go back to Sedona and try to find someone to sublet one of the rooms in the house we were renting," she replied. "I can't afford it without Brant's income, and I really don't want to move. We were lucky enough to find the place—it's a little cottage in Oak Creek Canyon, on the banks of the creek—and I don't want to let it go. I know I wouldn't be able to find anything half as nice on my own."

I hoped she could find someone. If the place was as inviting as she made it sound, she probably wouldn't have too much trouble. For a moment, I wondered if I should offer to float her rent for the next month, just to help her along until she found a roommate. Then I decided I probably should let it go. The first of September was three weeks away, and so that meant Sasha still had the bulk of the month to locate a roommate...and three weeks before she had to make rent. Helping out with Brant was one thing; I got the impression that anything else would feel too much like charity. Even so, I knew I'd be quick to help if she should ask.

Janice returned and said that Sasha could come back the next morning to pick up Brant's ashes. This concrete evidence that he was truly gone made her pale a little, but she nodded resolutely and said she'd be in around ten.

With that matter handled, we went out to the parking lot. Sasha paused by the driver's door of Brant's Subaru, expression diffident. "I don't know how to thank you for all this—" she began, but I waved a hand.

"It's fine," I said. "I wanted to help. What are you going to do now?"

"Go back to the hotel and regroup," she responded. "I have a bunch of calls to make. Then I'm probably going to watch TV and try not to think about much of anything."

That sounded like a good plan. I told her to call me if she needed anything, that I'd be at the store until five but would be reachable by cell after that.

"I'll be okay," she said. "I suppose if you hear anything important on the voice recorder, let me know."

"I will," I promised. Despite the muggy warmth of the afternoon, a little chill moved down my spine.

I really didn't want to listen to that thing… but I'd promised her I would.

We said goodbye after that, and both got in our cars and drove off to our separate destinations. The whole way back to the store, that chill stayed with me.

I had a bit of a reprieve until the store closed at five, but after that, I'd have to sit down and play the recording.

I had no idea what I'd find.

9

Cat With a Past

THE THREATENING WEATHER SEEMED TO KEEP most of the casual shoppers away, or even the not-so-casual ones; the person who'd been peeking in the store window early that afternoon never returned, and I didn't have a single shopper. I tried to keep myself busy by tidying up and putting in a couple of online orders for new merchandise, but even with those minor activities to distract me a bit, I didn't think I'd ever had a day that dragged as badly as this one. No texts from Calvin, either, which told me he must still be off chasing meth dealers.

At least one of us was doing something useful with their time.

As boring as my afternoon had been, I still took my time closing up. The extra weight of the mini-recorder in my purse was a reminder that I had an unpleasant task ahead of me.

But as much as I dallied, I was still back up in my apartment by ten minutes after five. Just as I was letting myself in, lightning flared, followed by a crack of thunder a few seconds later.

I hoped that wasn't an omen.

Archie was nowhere to be found. Or rather, I didn't bother to go in search of him, but figured he must be sleeping in the office, or maybe in the hallway on the thick wool runner he sometimes preferred to his bed, or even the rug in front of the washer/dryer unit in my tiny laundry room. His internal clock was impeccable, though, and so I knew he'd be out around six to start asking about his dinner.

I took my purse over to the dining room table and sat down, then plucked out the voice recorder and paused there for a moment, staring at it. My powers of psychometry—getting psychic impressions from objects—weren't as strong as my powers of divination, but sometimes I could get flashes from things, and I figured I might as well give it a try.

Nothing pinged my inner eye. The recorder just felt like a block of metal and plastic.

Of course it couldn't be that easy.

I blew out a breath. *Just turn it on,* I told myself. *You can't sit here all evening like an idiot.*

Maybe not…but there was also no law about getting myself a glass of pinot grigio to fortify myself for the coming ordeal.

Glad of the chance to delay for a couple of minutes, I got up from my chair and went into the kitchen to get the bottle of wine out of the refrigerator. I'd opened it a few days earlier, so I figured it was probably a good thing to have another glass now before the wine got too oxidized.

Having rationalized my actions, I returned to the dining room table, glass of pinot grigio in hand. I took a sip and then another, and figured I was now duly strengthened for the task ahead.

I pressed the Play button. To my surprise, Brant's voice came out of the tiny speaker…along with a cacophony of screeches and low, guttural moans. The hair on the back of my neck stood up, but I forced myself to listen intently, to focus on Brant's words and not the tumult in the background.

He was speaking in a low murmur, probably so he could avoid disturbing my mother and Tom, who I knew had gone back to bed at that point. Because of that, it was hard to hear everything he was saying, although I jacked up the sound on the recorder a few notches.

"The phenomena partially follow the classic pattern, occurring between midnight and 3 a.m.," he said. "However, there was also an incident around noon today, lasting for approximately ten minutes, and another around six. Not sure what to make of that. The manifestations appear to be mainly auditory, as you can hear in the background. If it's confirmed that this is truly a demonic infestation, then I might need to call Neil to handle it. But I want to gather more data before I make that determination, especially since the phenomena—so far, at least—appear to be purely auditory."

He sounded crisp and matter-of-fact, and not at all put off by the fact that it sounded as if a whole hellish chorus of demons had decided to descend on the stairwell and wail away.

And who was Neil? Did Brant know an exorcist, someone he kept on speed dial in case a particular situation got a little too out of hand?

I filed that question away to ask Sasha later if necessary.

"What on earth is that noise?"

Archie, standing at the edge of the apartment's small dining area, his nose scrunched in disgust and his tail flicking wildly.

"Sorry," I said as I hit the button to stop the playback. "It's a recording from the night that researcher died investigating the demons at my parents' house."

"It's dreadful," Archie declared.

I couldn't really argue with him on that one. Actually, it had been a relief to shut the darn thing off. "Well, demons aren't exactly known for their melodious voices."

The cat came closer to the dining table, then jumped up on one of the chairs. In the past, I'd told him to stay away from the furniture in there, since no one appreciates cat hair as a garnish to their meals, but right then, I was glad of the company. Listening to that recording had creeped me out even more than I'd thought it would.

"Why are you listening to it?" Archie asked, sounding genuinely curious.

I reached for my glass of pinot grigio and took a sip. Overhead, thunder crackled again, and in the next moment, rain began to pour down outside.

Looking at the deluge, I hoped my mother and Tom were safely back at the house by now. I didn't want to think about them driving around in that. Then again, I wasn't sure the word "safe" could be applied to a house infested with beings that could make the kind of noises I'd heard on the recording a moment earlier.

"I'm hoping there might be something on here that will tell me what really happened to Brant Thoreau," I told Archie.

He cocked his furry gray head. "I thought you said he fell down the stairs."

"He did. But was it an accident, or was he pushed?"

The cat didn't seem to have an answer to that question, so he lifted a paw and began licking it vigorously. I sipped some more pinot grigio and then started playing the recording again.

"...the sounds seem to be originating mainly from the stairwell. In fact...." Brant stopped speaking then, even as the demonic noises seemed to come to a crescendo.

Underneath the racket, though, was a sound that might have been an "oof," or maybe just him letting out a breath. Immediately afterward came a *thunk,* and then a series of thuds that culminated in a sharp crack, followed by an ominous silence.

I winced. It didn't take Sherlock Holmes to figure out what those sounds probably were—Brant Thoreau falling to his death on the Bigelow mansion's steep stairs.

Even Archie flinched a little. "That couldn't have been good," he remarked.

"No, it wasn't," I replied. Unfortunately, I hadn't heard any sounds on the recording that came across as anything more than a man suffering a tragic fall. No noises of demons screeching as they attacked...nothing that appeared to remotely be a scuffle. Now I understood why Chief Lewis had been okay with returning the voice recorder to Sasha—there was nothing on it to indicate anything except an awful accident.

Well, except those demonic noises clamoring in the background, but I had a feeling he'd written those off as bad plumbing or something similarly prosaic. Henry Lewis was not the sort of man who wanted to admit there was more to the world than met the eye.

I suppose I could have played the recording again with the sound turned up even louder, just in case I'd missed something, but I didn't know if I could endure listening to those dreadful noises again. Instead, I pushed the recorder away and reached for my wine.

"You seem somewhat melancholy," Archie said.

Was that sympathy I heard in his voice?

No, I must have been imagining things.

"It's always sad when someone dies too young," I replied. "And I hate that this happened in the house that my mother and Tom just bought. They should be enjoying it, not trying to stay away because a man died there recently…and because it might just happen to be infested with demons."

"You truly believe that about the demons?"

"You have a better explanation?"

Archie's tailed swished back and forth, and his

whiskers twitched. "Not really. I have to admit that I was rather surprised when you mentioned something supernatural was happening at the Bigelow house. It was always quite a serene place."

I blinked at him. "You've been there?"

"Yes," he said calmly. "Amanda Gardner—née Bigelow—was on the board of trustees for the local school district. She was the one who interviewed me for my position."

"A-ha!" I exclaimed, and Archie blinked at me, his expression seeming to indicate that he thought I'd lost my mind once and for all.

"Whatever was that about?"

"I just *knew* you had to be a teacher," I said. Ah, sweet vindication. Well, being a psychic did tend to give me good instincts about people. "English?"

"History," he replied.

Okay, so I wasn't batting a thousand. Still, I'd gotten the big part right.

"Born in September?" I asked.

That question got me a blink. "The ninth, actually."

I smiled and picked up my wine so I could have a celebratory swallow.

"Is there anything else you'd like to know?" Archie inquired, tone now a little sour.

"Lots, actually," I replied. "You've been

hanging out here for quite some time now, but you haven't told me very much about yourself."

He licked a paw, then rubbed it along the edge of one ear. When he spoke, he sounded more annoyed than usual. "Perhaps that's because my past is a painful subject, considering all this." He waved the same paw he'd just used to groom his ear as if to indicate his feline form, then hunkered down on the seat of the dining room chair where he was perched.

While I could understand Archie's reluctance to discuss his former life, I figured I might as well try to press on. "But maybe if I knew more about you, I'd be in a better position to help you get rid of your curse. Did you ever think of that?"

Judging by the way he blinked his big golden eyes at me just then, I got the impression that he hadn't. He was silent for a second or two before asking, "What else did you want to know?"

"Place and time of birth?" I inquired hope-fully. Yes, he'd just confirmed that he was a Virgo, but I needed those other details in order to work up a really comprehensive chart for him.

"Chicago, Illinois," he said. "Thursday, September ninth, 1920. I don't know the exact time…my mother said I was born just as the sun was coming up."

That would work. I could check online to see exactly when sunrise on that fateful day so long ago had occurred. And then I'd feed all the numbers into my favorite astrology website to get Archie's vitals. Yes, I could do it the longhand way using an ephemeris, but online was so much quicker and easier.

"How'd you end up in Globe?" I asked. It seemed like an awfully long way from Chicago. And it wasn't as though he'd settled down in an established city like Phoenix or Flagstaff, but a dinky little town out in the middle of nowhere.

"Does this third degree mean I'll get an extra salmon treat this evening?"

"Whatever you want," I promised.

He tilted his head. "I had asthma," he said. "I was 4F when the war came—you do know what that means, don't you?"

Since I didn't much like the condescension in his voice, I replied, my tone arch, "Medical exemption?"

"Yes." Judging by the grouchiness of that single word, I guessed he was annoyed that I hadn't proven my ignorance once again. "I was in college when the war broke out, so I was able to continue since I couldn't serve on active duty. Afterward, my health worsened, and a doctor suggested that I should move out west where the air was dryer. That was when I began actively looking for employment in Arizona or New Mexico or California. The job at the high school came up, so I traveled out here to interview for it, and that's how I met Amanda Gardner. She had the interview at her home—and I can assure you that there were no demonic goings-on while she lived there."

Of course there hadn't been, just as there hadn't been during the long decades when Hank and Nora Anders had owned the property. I absolutely refused to believe that the presence of my mother and her husband could have triggered a demonic attack—they were far too nice for that—so there had to be something else going on here.

Even if I couldn't begin to figure out what that "something" might be. One heck of a detective I was.

When I didn't say anything right away, Archie remarked, "I fail to see how knowing any of this can help you return me to my human form."

At the moment, I didn't, either. But knowledge was always a good thing, since you never knew when a particular tidbit might come in handy.

Something occurred to me then. "Aren't you worried that if I do turn you human again, you'll be an old man? I mean, you'd be more than a hundred years old."

His ears flattened. Voice prim, he responded, "I have been in this cat body for decades. It has never aged. I believe that when I become human again, I will look as I was when that witch first cursed me. I was thirty-four years old, with most of my life still ahead of me."

Thirty-four. It was hard to fathom that Archie —who always reminded me of a fussy old maid— had been only a few years older than I when he had his human form stripped from him. No wonder he was cranky.

"And you'll get that life back," I said. "Or at least, *a* life. Things have changed a lot since"—I paused to do the mental math—"1954."

"So I've noticed," he observed dryly. "But even being forced to live in the twenty-first century is preferable to being stuck in this cat's body for all eternity. Speaking of which, it's nearly six o'clock. I hope you're not going to get so wrapped up in this 'investigation' of yours that you forget to set out my dinner."

"I feed you at six-thirty," I pointed out.

"Just a reminder."

I shook my head. "You have nothing to worry about, Archie. Just one more listen-through, and then I'll get on it."

That announcement made him get up from the chair and drop gracefully to the floor. "Then I'll wait in the office until you're done. I have no desire to listen to that ruckus all over again."

He stalked off toward the back of the apartment, tail in the air.

I don't feel like listening to it again, either, I thought. *But some of us don't have a choice.*

Feeling resigned, I pulled the recorder toward me and hit the Play button again.

Well, hot damn, I thought as I stared at Archie's chart. *We've got a whole lot of Virgo up in here.*

Because it wasn't just his sun in Virgo—it was also his ascending sign, along with Mercury, Jupiter, and Saturn, a grouping of planets that was known in astrology as a stellium. No wonder he wanted everything to be exactly just so. And yes, of course there was much more to the sign of the Virgin than a predilection toward neatness and order, but still. True node in Scorpio; it didn't surprise me that one of the karmic lessons Archie needed to learn from this life was to be a little less rigid and to embrace change.

Maybe he'd be able to do that once he wasn't a cat anymore.

That day seemed far off, though, and I still had the issue of the demons infesting the Bigelow mansion to deal with. A second listen of the recording, while uncomfortable, hadn't yielded any further useful data. The noises from the demons didn't seem to have changed materially from the time when Brant Thoreau was listening to them to the horrible moment when he tumbled down the stairs. If any of them were the culprits, they'd been pretty stealthy about it.

I set aside my laptop and reached for the bowl of soup I'd heated up for my dinner. Because I was planning a big dinner for Calvin and Tom and my mother, I'd decided to take it easy during this quiet evening in. Or not so quiet; unlike a lot of monsoon storms, which did their business and then moved on, the one that had parked itself over Globe in the late afternoon seemed ready to stick around for a while.

Archie had eaten his dinner and then gone back to his bed in the office. Something about his manner seemed almost diffident, as if he wasn't quite sure he'd done the right thing by revealing so much of his past to me. I appreciated that he'd opened up, though, because even if I didn't quite know what to do with any of that information at just this moment, I at least felt as if I understood him a little better. Had it been difficult for him to sit out World War 2 as people he knew fought and died, or had he been glad that his asthma had ensured he wouldn't perish on the battlefields of France or in the jungles of the Philippines?

I wouldn't ask, mostly because I had a feeling he was done with confessions for the moment. Having his astrological chart would help me almost as much as picking his brain...and it would be a lot easier to work with.

My cell phone rang, and I set down my soup spoon and picked up the phone.

Calvin.

"Hey," he said, voice warm, sending happy little thrills all over me. "How are you doing?"

"I'm fine," I replied. "But not as fine as I would be if you were here."

"I know," he said. "I wish I were there, too. But at least it looks as if we've got this meth thing pretty well locked down, so I'm hoping that means there won't be anything to keep me from coming to dinner tomorrow night."

"Well, that's something," I said. "You weren't doing anything too dangerous, were you?"

He chuckled. "Doing dangerous stuff is part of my job, you know. But in this case, it was mostly chasing down a bunch of *Breaking Bad* wannabes. They weren't too organized, and they weren't armed, and now they're all sitting in lock-up awaiting arraignment. That was probably my excitement quota for the month, unless you count helping Hector Salazar get his cows off our range —they're always busting through the fences."

I smiled, even though Calvin couldn't see my expression. "Yes, that sounds like a real thrill a minute."

"I much prefer busting cows to busting meth

heads, that's for sure." He paused before asking, "Anything new on the demon front?"

A sigh I couldn't quite hold back slipped from between my lips. "Not a lot. I've got the recording Brant Thoreau made the night he died, but I didn't hear anything on it that offered any kind of a real clue."

"It's still quiet at the house?"

"I guess so," I answered. "Or at least, I haven't heard anything from my mother, so I assume that's good news. She and Tom spent most of the day out, but I'm sure they must be back at the house now. I was planning to call in the morning to check on them."

"And they know to get out if things get dicey?"

"I'm sure they do," I said. "But I went over there with Sasha earlier today to get Brant's things and his car, and it was absolutely quiet. More than that, it felt almost…serene. It was strange."

Calvin was quiet for a second or two. Then he said, "What do you make of it?"

"I honestly don't know," I confessed. "Something about this whole situation feels off, but I can't puzzle out what it might be."

"Well, I'm sure you'll figure it out," he replied, his voice mellow, reassuring. "I've never met anyone with better instincts than you."

The praise cheered me up, even as I thought he might be overstating things a bit. Sure, I couldn't deny that my psychic powers gave me insights which might elude other people who didn't have the same extrasensory gifts, but I still couldn't stop myself from thinking that I didn't yet have a handle on what was going on at the Bigelow mansion.

"Here's hoping," I said.

"You'll do fine," he told me. "Gotta go—miss you."

He hung up then, and I held the phone for a moment before gently putting it down on the coffee table. I missed him, too, more than I wanted to admit. Our relationship had taken a quantum leap a few days earlier, but I hadn't seen much of him since then, thanks to his work and the goings-on at my mother and Tom's place. That he'd come right out and told me he missed me meant more than I could say.

Well, I'd see Calvin the next evening. That was twenty-four more hours than I wanted to spend away from him, but at least we had firm plans to see each other.

I supposed I had to be content with that.

The rain stuck around for the rest of the evening, and I went to sleep listening to the soft *tap-tap* of raindrops pattering against my bedroom window...only to be awakened a few hours later by my phone ringing on the nightstand.

I reached for it at once, my body thrumming with adrenaline. Calls in the middle of the night were never a good thing…especially when your mother and her husband were currently living in a house that might or might not be infested with demons.

Without looking at the screen, I put the phone to my ear. "Hello?"

"Selena."

Tom's voice. He sounded shaken.

"What's the matter?"

"It's happening again."

I sat bolt upright in bed. "Are you okay?" I strained to hear any sound of demonic predations, but the background seemed eerily quiet.

"We're all right. We're sitting out in the car because your mother didn't want to stay inside."

Well, I couldn't really blame her for that. "I'll be right over."

"You don't need to do that—"

"Yes, I do," I cut in. "I told you I'd help, and I meant it."

"It doesn't matter," he said, sounding more tired than I'd ever heard him before. "We're going to stay in a hotel."

Maybe that was the smart thing to do, but I hated the thought of them simply running away.

"Please, just give me a few minutes. I'll be there as fast as I can."

A pause as there seemed to be a muffled convo between Tom and my mother. Then he said, "All right. We'll wait."

"Thank you. I'm hanging up now."

I ended the call and put the phone on my nightstand, then got out of bed and grabbed a pair of jeans and my Keds. Since I'd been wearing a T-shirt to sleep in, I just pulled it up out of the way so I could slide a bra on underneath.

Thus ready to go, I slipped out of the bedroom. To my annoyance, Archie was sitting in the hall, wide awake.

"Let me guess," he said. "Another demon emergency."

"Something like that," I replied. "I'll be fine. Go back to sleep."

"I hope this doesn't mean you'll miss feeding me breakfast," he remarked in ominous tones.

"I'll do my best. Gotta go."

I hurried over to the dining room table and grabbed my purse, then was out the door. From somewhere behind me, I heard an irritated hiss.

Say a prayer for me, Archie, I thought as I locked the door. *Because if this goes sideways, you're going to have much bigger problems than a missed meal....*

10

Getting Out of Dodge

EVEN THOUGH THE RAIN HAD STOPPED, THE streets were still slick and treacherous. My instincts were all screaming at me to hurry, but I knew I wouldn't be of much use to my mother and Tom if I managed to wrap my car around an electrical pole in my haste.

Somehow, I managed to obey the speed limit...mostly...and pulled into the now-familiar gravel driveway less than ten minutes after I'd left my apartment. The door to the garage bay where Tom had been parking his Cayenne stood open, and as soon as I pulled up and came to a stop, he and my mother emerged.

Their faces looked extra pale in the darkness, since the only illumination was some landscape lights and one of those motion-activated security fixtures bolted to the garage eaves. They were both fully dressed, so at least they'd had the presence of mind to put on some clothes before they fled the place.

"What happened?" I asked.

"The same thing as the last few times," my mother replied. She didn't seem all that relieved to see me, was actually frowning, as if my presence had only given her one more thing to worry about. "Pounding in the walls…all those horrible voices screaming and laughing. But then…."

Her words trailed off, and she shot an anxious look up at Tom. "Then it got worse," he said.

"Worse how?" Honestly, I was hard pressed to think how anything could be worse than listening to that hellish cacophony.

I was about to find out.

"Smells," he said. "Horrible smells. It was so bad we could barely breathe. That was when we realized we had to get out. So we got dressed and grabbed our things, and headed out to the garage."

I glanced away from him, directing my gaze toward the house. Lights showed in several of the windows, seeming to signal that my mother and Tom hadn't bothered to shut anything down as they fled the place. Not that I could blame them; I would've wanted to keep the lights on, too.

It was all eerily quiet now—or rather, if the demons were making a ruckus, the sound wasn't traveling as far as the garage. I suppose that made sense; despite the monsoon storm earlier, the night was still warm, and now a little muggy, thanks to all the rain. Most likely, my mother and Tom had the windows shut and were running the air conditioning, which meant there was a perfectly logical reason for why I couldn't hear anything.

"Guess I'd better go check it out," I said, and my mother made a muffled sound of alarm.

"You shouldn't go in there," Tom told me.

I shrugged. Whether he believed the casual act, I didn't know, but it was just as important to me to pretend this was another day at the office as it was for him to believe me. Honestly, I couldn't think of many things I had less inclination to do than walk into that house. However, I'd promised to help, and I'd come all the way over here, and so it was silly to stand out by the garage and do nothing.

"It'll be all right," I assured him. "I just want to listen to what's going on. I don't plan to go upstairs."

Those words seemed to relieve Tom a little bit —he hesitated, then glanced down at my mother and said, "That sounds like it should be okay."

"I don't know," she replied. Despite the muggy warmth of the night, she had on a sweatshirt and was hugging her arms around herself, as if she'd picked up a chill she couldn't dispel. Maybe even her hot flashes weren't enough to keep her warm in this sort of situation. "I don't think it's worth it, Selena. It's just a house."

Maybe that was true, but now my professional pride was involved. I needed to know just what the heck was going on in there.

"I'll be careful," I said. "And I'll be out here at the first hint of any trouble. I've got my running shoes on, see?"

And I lifted one foot to show off my lime green Keds.

That gesture earned me a weak smile. "If you're sure…."

"I'm sure," I said firmly. "Just wait here. I'll be back in five."

Before either of them could offer any further protests, I turned and headed up the flagstone path to the front porch. As I approached, I had the stray worry that maybe they'd locked the door as they left, and I'd be forced to head back and get the key.

But no—when I put my hand on the knob, it turned easily enough.

I pulled in a breath and stepped inside.

And immediately thanked the Goddess that I'd gotten a mouthful of damp night air while I was standing on the porch, because I definitely didn't want to breathe in any of the fetid odor that immediately surrounded me. It smelled like a wet skunk had rolled in road kill and then rubbed its stinking fur over every surface in the house.

I wanted to gag but somehow held it together. From the stairwell came the same moans and screams and horrible giggling laughs that I'd heard before, only even louder this time, more strident. Those sounds were interspersed with pounding noises that sounded as though they were emanating from inside the walls.

Even though I wanted to turn and run, I made myself take a step forward, and then another. Maybe it would have been better if I'd been brandishing a cross in one hand and a vial of holy water in the other, but all I had with me was the jar of moon water I'd grabbed as I left the apartment.

It would have to do.

I fished it out of my purse and unscrewed the lid, and took a quick breath. The air seemed to stink even worse this time, and I swallowed. I honestly didn't know how long I'd be able to hold out in here.

Heart pounding, I approached the stairwell. All right, I had promised my mother and Tom that I wouldn't go upstairs, but I figured it should be safe enough to stop in front of the first step.

"This isn't your home!" I cried out. "By all the

gods and spirits, by all the powers of the four quarters, I banish you from this place!"

And I splashed some moon water onto the banister and the steps.

I didn't know what I'd been expecting. Some kind of a reaction, even if it was derisive laughter at my puny efforts.

But nothing happened. The moaning and the shrieks and the giggles continued, and the pounding still came from inside the walls. It was like I wasn't there at all.

Which maybe was a good thing. If the demons were ignoring me, that meant they probably weren't inclined to do me bodily harm the way they had poor Brant Thoreau.

"I mean it!" I called out. "Leave this place, or I'll come back with the big guns!"

Exactly which big guns, I wasn't sure. Maybe the "Neil" person Brant had mentioned on his recording. I somehow doubted the priest at the local Catholic church would be too interested in lending a hand—the couple of times I'd met him, he'd seemed like a stuffy individual, not the sort of person to get involved in an exorcism.

Or maybe he just hadn't approved of the pentacle I had hanging around my neck at the time.

Everything went dead quiet. For a second, I just stood there, goggling at the sudden silence.

Could it really be that easy?

A clock somewhere on the first floor chimed, a single peal.

One a.m.

Had the demons all decided to clock out and go for a drink somewhere?

I put one foot on the bottom step and hesitated. Part of me wanted to go upstairs, or at least to the landing, just to see what was going on, while the other kept telling me to get the hell out of there.

Also, just because the noise had stopped didn't mean the awful stench had gone away. It was still everywhere, thick enough that I was surprised I couldn't see it hanging in the air like some kind of horrible fog.

Discretion was the better part of valor, after all.

I turned away from the stairs and headed out the front door, then closed it behind me and let myself pause to pull in some deep, heavenly breaths of untainted night air. Once I thought I was sufficiently recovered, I headed down the porch steps and along the walkway to the garage where my mother and Tom were waiting.

They gazed at me expectantly as I approached. "It stopped," I said simply.

"What happened?" my mother asked, astonishment clear in her face despite the uncertain light from the security fixture overhead.

"I don't know," I said. "The sounds were terrible. I tried some moon water, and that didn't make any difference. Then I said I was going to bring in the big guns, and it all stopped immediately."

"'Big guns'?" Tom repeated.

"Just an idea I had," I told him. "Mostly an empty threat. But it seemed to work…or maybe it was just a coincidence. Anyway, it's quiet again. Unfortunately, that smell doesn't seem like it's going anywhere."

"Which is why we're still going to a hotel," my mother said. "There's no way in the world we can sleep in that. Tomorrow…well, tomorrow we'll figure out what to do next."

I wanted to argue with her, but I could see the exhaustion in both her and Tom's faces, and knew they needed to go someplace where they could get some real rest. "Sure," I said. "That sounds like a good plan. Just call me when you're up."

"We will." She stepped closer and gave me a quick hug. "Thanks, hon. Going in there was very brave of you. But I think we'll all do better after a decent night's sleep."

That sounded like good advice, so I nodded, asked her again to call me when they were awake, and headed off to my car. As I pulled out of the driveway, I couldn't help yawning.

Yes, I needed to sleep. But first, I was going to take a shower and wash my hair…and hope that would get rid of the demon stink.

"We're going back to L.A.," my mother said.

I stared at her blankly. She and Tom had agreed to meet me for breakfast at The Flatiron, but suddenly the restaurant's excellent hash browns tasted like cardboard. "You're what?"

Tom put his hand over hers and gave it a reassuring squeeze. "We're both tired, Selena," he said. "This was supposed to be a mini vacation for us, but it's turned out to be a nightmare from beginning to end."

"Except for getting to see you, of course," my mother put in quickly. "I'm thrilled to have had the chance to see where you live and get a real-life peek at your shop…and to meet Calvin. But Tom is right—we're tired, and there doesn't seem to be any way to get the house livable, so we're going to go back home and regroup and decide what to do next."

"There are other things I could try—" I began, but she shook her head.

"Someone died in there, Selena. I can't forget

that—and I certainly don't want to put anyone else in harm's way."

I closed my mouth without saying anything. My mother was right—Brant Thoreau had lost his life in that house. Even if I were able to track down the "Neil" from the recording, did I want to take the chance of him meeting a similar fate?

"Nothing firm has been decided yet," Tom put in. "But there's definitely no point in staying in that house. It clearly doesn't want us there."

Well, *something* didn't, that much was clear. I doubted the problem lay with the house itself, though. Still, if Tom and my mother were determined to go back to Southern California, there wasn't a lot I could do to change their minds.

"When are you leaving?" I asked, not bothering to keep the resignation out of my tone.

"Just as soon as we're done here," my mother replied. Her expression was apologetic.

"But…you were supposed to come over for dinner tonight."

She reached over and patted my hand. "I know, sweetie, and I'm sorry about that. Give our apologies to Calvin—I'm sure he'll understand."

Being Calvin, of course he would. But I'd bought supplies to make an Italian dinner for four. Oh, well…I'd just be eating leftover lasagna for the next week. And of course, I'd send a care package home with Calvin, too.

"Okay," I said, knowing that arguing the point any further would just upset my mother. A thought occurred to me, and I asked, "Can you leave a key to the house for me, though? I'm not quite ready to give up on this."

"I don't want you putting yourself in any danger—" she began.

"I'm sure Selena will be careful," Tom said, interrupting her. "And really, it's just smart to have someone local with a key in case of an emergency." He extricated a key ring from his pocket, then pulled off a shiny new brass key and handed it to me. "This only unlocks the deadbolt on the front door, but that's enough to get you in. We did go back this morning and turn off the air conditioning and the lights, so there's no immediate reason for you to go over there."

No reason except a mystery I couldn't seem to solve. However, I took the key and slipped it onto my own key ring without comment. As I reached for my coffee, my mother spoke again.

"Please only use that key in case of emergency. I really think everyone should stay out of the house for the time being."

She knew me way too well. I'd already been plotting how to run over there and do a quick check of everything before I had to open the shop. I swallowed some coffee and said, "You can't leave it like this forever, Mom."

"I'm not," she replied. "Like I said before, we're just going away so we can get some perspective on the situation and figure out what to do next."

"Are you going to sell the house?" I asked. "Because I doubt anyone's going to want to buy the place with this mess going on."

The two of them traded a glance, and I got a brief flash of yellow spikes radiating out from my mother's aura before they disappeared. Yellow often indicated guilt, which seemed to indicate that they had already discussed the subject of selling the Bigelow mansion but didn't want to tell me because they weren't sure how I'd react.

"We're keeping our options open," Tom said. That was all he said, and I could tell he wanted me to drop the subject.

Which I did. They were adults and would do what they needed to do. Maybe they'd realize soon enough that the house really wasn't sellable as-is, and so we'd have to investigate bringing in an expert to try to cleanse the place.

An uncomfortable silence fell as we all sipped coffee or returned to our neglected breakfasts and tried to act as though all of this was normal. It wasn't, of course, but I knew my mother wanted this last shared meal of ours to be at least somewhat pleasant.

Afterward, I walked them out to their car, and

gave them both hugs goodbye. My mother returned my hug with unaccustomed fierceness, saying, "Maybe you can come visit us. I'd love for you to be home for Christmas."

I made a noncommittal sound, partly because, although the house she and Tom shared was very nice, it certainly had never been *my* home, and partly because I really wanted to be in Globe for my first Christmas there. Josie had told me that snow was a rare occasion but did happen from time to time. Just the thought of being able to watch the snow falling, my head pillowed on Calvin's shoulder, a Christmas tree glimmering in the background, was enough to make me sure that I didn't want to be anywhere else for the holidays.

And okay, I was a practicing pagan and didn't really celebrate Christmas—I focused my holiday energies on the winter solstice—but Christmas trees were kind of universal.

My mother seemed to sense my reluctance, because she didn't push it. She only gave me a final squeeze before letting go, and then she and Tom got into his SUV. I stood off to one side and waved as they backed out of their parking space and then headed out to the highway.

For a minute, I lingered there, watching them go, feeling a bit melancholy. So much still felt up in the air, something I didn't care for very much. Probably because of my North Node in Capricorn, although I realized I had to accept that was sometimes how the world worked.

I got in my car. The key to the house felt like a lump of glowing plutonium in my purse. I knew I needed to resist its radioactive glow—my mother had all but forbidden me to go back to the Bigelow mansion unless there was an emergency. Exactly what such an emergency might constitute, I wasn't really sure.

Still....

Oh, the hell with it.

I pointed the car east, but passed the downtown section and my store, knowing I was going to make a liar out of my little "be back at" sign and telling myself it wasn't a big deal. Most of the merchants on Broad Street had a very, well, broad definition of what "on time" exactly meant. If I was a half hour late, it certainly wouldn't be the end of the world.

The storms of the day before were gone as if they'd never been. Above, a cheerful sun shone out of the clear blue sky, and the unexpected green of monsoon season made this little corner of Arizona look far more lush than I'd ever expected it to be. On a day like this, it was almost possible to forget what I'd heard...and smelled...in the Bigelow mansion the previous night.

Almost.

In that bright sunlight, I could see the beginnings of ruts from all the rain forming in the property's gravel driveway. I supposed there was someone I could call to come out and make sure it was properly manicured, but if my mother and Tom really were thinking of unloading the place, they might not care. I really hoped they wouldn't take a bath on it, though.

I didn't bother to pull up all the way to the garage. Instead, I stopped the car close to the spot where the flagstone path met the driveway and got out. A warm, fresh breeze caught my loose hair, and I breathed in the scent of roses from the gardens nearby. This really was a gorgeous spot… as long as I made myself forget what was going on inside the house itself.

Key in hand, I made my way up the path to the front door. The lock was a little sticky, but I got inside soon enough. Almost at once, the same stench I'd smelled last night hit my nose. I didn't think it was quite as strong as before, although that hardly mattered when it was still pretty awful.

Trying to hold my breath, I hurried into the living room and threw open the windows, then did the same in the dining room and the small parlor off to the side where a baby grand piano sat. Almost at once, the same breeze that had played with my hair a few moments earlier rushed through the place, pushing out the terrible smell. It wasn't gone entirely, but I thought that if the windows stayed open for an hour or so, every-thing should be back to normal.

Not that I planned on staying here for a whole hour.

All around me, the house was silent. The only sounds were the rustle of leaves coming in through the open windows, and the trill of a bird from time to time. Maybe my ears were deceiving me, but it sure seemed as though the demons had decided to take the morning off.

I headed toward the stairs, then set my jaw and made myself ascend the first step, and then the next. The whole time, I maintained a death grip on the banister. If something intended to come along and send me plunging down the stairs just as it had done to Brant Thoreau, it was going to have to pry my fingers loose first.

However, as I paused on the landing, I once again got the sense that there was nothing here. With the stink receding, the place felt like an ordinary house. All right, an ordinary perfectly restored four-thousand-square-foot Victorian mansion, but still.

I stood there quietly, letting myself absorb the home's energies. Nothing sent up any alarms. Nothing gave me that odd tickly/creepy sensation I usually got when I entered a house haunted by spirits who should have moved on to the next world.

Just what the heck was going on here?

With one hand, I reached out and touched the vibrantly patterned wallpaper that lined the stairwell. It was cool and smooth under my fingertips. I almost expected one of those terrible thumps to rock the plaster I touched, but everything stayed quiet.

Maybe the demons really had moved on, now that they knew they'd succeeded in driving my mother and Tom out of the house.

Problem was, I could call the two of them right now and tell them their house was fine, and I doubted that would change anything. They'd already been lured back to this place once by a false illusion of peace and quiet, and they wouldn't fall for that again.

Which meant...which meant I probably had to get used to the idea of them selling the place. Honestly, since they'd only owned it for a week, it wasn't as though I could claim I was attached to the house. I suppose it was more that I'd come to like the idea of my mother and Tom sharing just a little of my life by staying here a few weeks out of the year.

Well, it wouldn't kill me to visit them in California, even if I didn't go back during the holidays. At least I didn't have to worry about Lucien Dumond coming after me if I set foot in the greater Los Angeles area.

I released a breath, and descended the stairs. Maybe I should have gone up to the second floor to snoop around, but I had a feeling doing so would only have been an additional waste of time and energy.

Still, I wasn't quite ready to let things go. I needed to do a little more digging…and I knew exactly who could help me unearth the information I was looking for.

11

Dinner for Two

But when I went in search of Josie at her office, I found it closed, with a note on the door that she was off in Phoenix for the day. What she was doing there, I had no idea, but clearly my questions would have to wait until the following morning.

So, I was only about twenty minutes late opening the shop. I'd already planned to close early in order to get home in enough time to start preparing dinner, but since it was early in the week, I wasn't expecting a lot of shoppers. On the drive back downtown, I'd also toyed with the idea of calling Calvin and canceling, but I realized doing that wouldn't serve any real purpose. I still had all the ingredients for the lasagna that needed to get used up, and delaying our dinner would only make them that much less fresh.

Instead, I texted him and said, *Looks like it's just you and me for dinner tonight. Will explain when I see you.*

He responded with, *Sorry to hear that...but looking forward to dinner for two.*

So was I.

The afternoon was a little busier than I expected, because a small tour bus that was traveling from Payson to Mesa stopped downtown and disgorged its passengers, giving them an hour to roam before they got back on the road. I racked up a decent number of sales and definitely felt cheerier than I had that morning.

At four I closed up and headed upstairs to the apartment. I'd already warned Archie that Calvin and I would be having a romantic dinner for two, and so the cat seemed grouchier than ever.

"I don't see why you can't go out to eat like normal people do," he remarked as I slid the sheets of lasagna noodles into a big saucepan to boil.

"I like to cook," I said, refusing to let him get to me. "I think cooking for people shows you care for them. Tell you what," I added so he wouldn't be able to get a word in edgewise, "when I turn you back into a man, I'll make you your favorite dish. Just tell me what you'd like."

"Beef Wellington," he replied promptly, and I lifted an eyebrow at him.

"Is that really your favorite, or do you just want me to make it because it's difficult?"

His ears twitched in annoyance. "It's my favorite, and I haven't had it for more than sixty years. The puff pastry...the gravy...the tender roast beef...." He trailed off there, golden eyes half closing in what I assumed was an ecstatic memory of the experience.

"Then Beef Wellington it is," I said.

"It's a deal." Archie stopped there before going on, "Make sure I can get out onto the balcony tonight. I don't want to be anywhere around should matters get too amorous."

"Not a problem," I told him. After all, I didn't want an audience if the evening turned hot and heavy once we were done with dinner. I supposed I should be glad that at least Archie was willing to meet me halfway, and wasn't putting his furry foot down and demanding absolutely no displays of affection between Calvin and me besides a good-night peck on the cheek.

Apparently satisfied with our arrangement, the cat headed off to get a late afternoon nap on the floor by the living room window, and I kept working away. Soon enough, it was time to actually assemble the lasagna, and at six o'clock, I popped it in the oven. I took advantage of the lull to go into the bedroom and change into something a little more appropriate for a romantic dinner for two, which in this case was a draped tank top and one of my sequined skirts from India. Other than the lasagna, I was making a tossed garden salad and some garlic bread, but both of those could wait until closer to dinnertime.

Once I was ready, I headed over to the living room window and cracked it wide enough to allow Archie to come and go. Doing so let in some warm damp air that fought with the A/C working away in the background, but I figured it was a small price to pay to ensure domestic tranquility. The cat was eating his dinner at the time, and came out afterward and inspected the window.

"Thank you," was all he said, but for Archie, that was being pretty mellow.

Soon enough after that, Calvin knocked on the door, and the cat promptly bailed. I would have been worried about him roaming around town after dark, but since he'd spent decades doing just that and seemed to have survived the experience just fine, I told myself to relax. Besides, this deep in town, he was probably safe from marauding coyotes and bobcats, with the biggest worry someone deciding to speed along Broad Street, which was limited to twenty-five miles an hour in the downtown section—a speed limit that only about a third of the town's population seemed to obey.

I opened the door to see Calvin in jeans and one of his dark-toned button-up shirts, this one in a nice eggplant shade. He held a bottle of wine in one hand.

"Hey," he said.

"Hey," I responded, and stepped out of the way so he could come into the apartment.

A quick kiss on one cheek—with a gleam in his dark eyes that told me the caress was only a down payment on future activities—and he handed over the bottle of wine. I looked down at the label and raised an eyebrow.

"'Chateau Tumbleweed'?" I asked.

"One of my favorite Arizona wineries," he said. "They're up in the Verde Valley, about twenty miles outside Sedona. I thought this sangiovese would be perfect with lasagna."

"I'm sure it will," I said. I went over to the dining room table and set the wine bottle down on it. "Why don't you go ahead and open that up? I'm just about to get everything out of the oven."

He nodded, and came over and picked up the corkscrew I'd left sitting out on the table. While he was occupied with opening the wine, I headed back into the kitchen and pulled the lasagna and garlic bread out of the oven, then brought them over to the dining room. I'd already set out hot pads to shield the table from the lasagna pan, so I put it down there.

Once everything was assembled, we both sat down, and Calvin poured us some wine. "To a quiet evening together," he said as he raised his glass.

After the tumult of the past few days, I could definitely drink to that. I clinked my glass against his, and said, "To quiet evenings."

We both drank, and then he asked, "Do you want to tell me what happened with your mother and Tom?"

I swallowed some more wine. He was right; it was really good. "There was another disturbance last night, and they both decided they'd had enough. They're probably already back in SoCal by now."

Calvin shook his head as he dished some lasagna for the both of us. "That's rough…but understandable. What do you think they're going to do with the place?"

"They haven't come right out and said it, but I have a feeling they're going to try to sell the house." I plucked a piece of garlic bread from the basket and then offered some to Calvin. He helped himself to a slice, and I added, "I just don't know how well that's going to work with everything so unresolved."

"Yeah, I could see that a house possessed by demons might be a hard sell."

I didn't bother to point out the difference between possessions and infestations. Tomato, to-mah-to. "And I also can't shake the feeling that something else is going on here, something else I just can't figure out."

"It'll come to you." He set down his fork and reached over so he could lightly stroke the back of my hand—a warm, reassuring touch that immediately made me feel better. "You're trying to help, so no sense in beating yourself up."

"You're right, of course." I smiled at him and sipped some more wine. "Okay, tell me more about Chateau Tumbleweed."

He sent me an answering grin, complete with friendly crinkles around his dark eyes. "There's not a lot to tell. They make great wine and have a tasting room in Clarkdale." A pause, and then he said, "You know, we should really plan a trip up to the Verde Valley sometime. We could spend a few days going to the various wineries in the area—there's actually a lot of them. And we could visit Sedona. That's supposed to be kind of a woo-woo place, isn't it?"

I wrinkled my nose at him. True, I used the term "woo-woo" myself from time to time, but it tended to get my hackles up when someone else said it. "Supposedly," I replied. "I think a lot of it has been kind of commercialized, though. Still, it would be fun to check out Sedona. The area is really beautiful, isn't it?"

"Yes," he said. "I've only driven through and haven't stayed there, but it is pretty amazing, the sort of place everyone should try to visit if they can."

That sounded like a great idea. I thought of how nice it would be to get away to a place where no one knew either one of us, where we could just be tourists and not have to worry about demon-infested houses or cursed cats or anything else.

I'd have to find a cat sitter for Archie, though. Maybe Hazel could help me out, since it would only be for a couple of days.

"Then let's put that on the tentative calendar," I replied. "What's a good time to visit there?"

"I think it can still be pretty hot in September," Calvin said. "But October is usually nice."

Did that comment mean he was anticipating a future for us that lasted into the fall? It sure sounded that way. I wasn't sure how to respond, mostly because my relationships back in L.A. tended to involve me tiptoeing around anything that sounded like making plans which extended beyond the end of the next week. Los Angeles men were notorious commitment-phobes.

It didn't seem as though I'd run into the same problem with Calvin.

As if guessing at my inner hesitation, he went on, in that calm, steady way of his, "I know I was planning for us to still be together in October. I hope you were, too."

I raised my eyes to meet his. "Yes, definitely."

A smile, and he leaned back in his chair. "Good. This is sort of uncharted territory for me, but I definitely don't want you to think I'm planning on bailing out."

"Even though your tribe isn't thrilled about us dating?"

His smile slipped a little, but he still replied, "I'm not sure that's the right way to phrase it. More like they're wary. Which I can understand."

"You didn't date at all when you were going to ASU?"

Because Calvin had told me a while back that he'd attended college in Tempe, getting a degree in criminal justice. He wasn't the first of his tribe to get a bachelor's, but still, it wasn't the norm for his people, either. They tended to stick close to home.

He chuckled at that question. "Like I had the time. I was commuting from here the whole time I was in college, and it was almost an hour and a half each way. Between the drive and the class load I was carrying, I didn't have much time for a social life. Also, what would have been the point? I knew none of those relationships would've gone anywhere."

"Oh," I said, which I knew was a weak response. If he hadn't been with anyone in college, and he'd never married, then exactly how had he gotten so…skilled?

"I met women at the casino," he said, as if in answer to my unspoken question. "People passing through. I wasn't going to live like a monk, and I didn't think it would be fair to have anything casual with one of the women in my tribe. They would have expected it to turn into something serious. I'm sure my mother would have been even more on my case if I didn't have my brothers and sisters and their families to keep her occupied. With half a dozen grandchildren and more on the way, it isn't as though she can exactly guilt me about being the only one of her friends without grandkids."

I smiled and shook my head, then reached for another piece of garlic bread. Thank God my mother had never given me grief about being unmarried and child-free. Since she looked so spectacularly good for her age, maybe she wasn't ready to be a grandmother yet.

Or maybe after getting a dose of Tom's spoiled-brat grandkids, she'd decided she was okay with not having any of her own.

However, I was pretty sure she'd be perfectly

fine with Calvin and me starting our own family, if and when that ever happened.

"Anyway," Calvin went on, as if guessing it might be a good idea to steer the conversation away from grandchildren…at least for the time being, "we should start planning a trip to the Verde Valley. There are a bunch of nice hotels in Sedona, or we could get an Airbnb in Cotton-wood or Jerome."

"What's Jerome?"

"It's a former mining town that's turned into kind of a funky, arty tourist attraction. Very off-beat. I think you'd like it."

Jerome definitely sounded like someplace I'd want to explore. I didn't want to stay in a glossy resort; I wanted someone's kitschy Airbnb.

"Let's try for Jerome," I said.

Calvin sent me a knowing smile, as if he'd already guessed I'd choose Jerome as our preferred destination. "It's a deal. Sometime next week, let's sit down with your laptop and get it figured out."

Our getaway destination settled, we went on to talk about our plans with Hazel and Chuck to go out to the movies sometime in the coming week, and whether we were going to stick with Globe's dinky little theater downtown or head out to Mesa or Gilbert to see something in a big place with stadium seating and all the perks.

The one thing we didn't discuss was the

Bigelow mansion and what my parents planned to do with it. That was a relief, even though I knew the house and its uninvited occupants were something that would have to be tackled sooner rather than later.

And after dinner, Calvin took me by the hand and kissed me, held me close…and I led him to the bedroom and shut the door.

After all, Archie had slipped out hours earlier, but a girl couldn't be too safe.

The next morning, I headed over to Josie's office early, hoping I could catch her before I had to open the shop. To my relief, she was there, putting together what looked like packets of materials for her latest listings. I'd sometimes wondered if there was really enough real estate turnover in tiny Globe to keep her occupied, but she did seem to be perpetually busy.

She was frowning, though, a frown that wiped itself away as soon as she looked up and saw me standing at the doorway to her office.

"Selena!" she exclaimed. "So good to see you!"

"I hope I'm not interrupting anything," I said.

My comment made her wave a hand in dismissal. "Oh, no. I'm just getting these listing materials ready for my next open house, but that's not until two days from now. You know how I like to be prepared."

That was true. She had to be one of the most organized people I'd ever met. "It looked like you were upset about something."

Josie paused there, hands resting on a stack of color laser-printed listing sheets. "Well, if you must know, I had something of a tussle with Miriam Jacobsen earlier."

The head of the local Chamber of Commerce? I knew that Josie had had a few run-ins with Ms. Jacobsen—Hazel referred to them as the irresistible force meeting the immovable object—but it seemed that in general, they tried to stay out of one another's orbits.

"What about?"

She sighed. "Oh, I simply said that I thought it would be a good idea to have costumed carolers for the festival of lights in December—you know, something to evoke the old pioneer and mining days of the town. But she said it wasn't a living history event and there was no reason to get so elaborate." The frown returned as she added, "You know, sometimes I think Miriam is actively going out of her way to keep people away from this town."

I made a sound of demurral, even though I privately thought Josie might be on to something there. Luckily, I'd mostly managed to avoid

Miriam, except for the one notable time when she came into the shop to take pictures for an updated Chamber of Commerce brochure. She managed to spend the entire time she was photographing the place looking as though she'd smelled something bad. Maybe she didn't like me, or she didn't like the idea of a pagan store right smack in the middle of Globe's quaint downtown. Whatever the reason, our interaction hadn't exactly been what you could call cordial.

"Oh, I suppose she just has her own views on how things should be managed," I said, and Josie sniffed.

"She has her own views, all right. Too bad that so many of them are dead wrong. She told me we simply didn't have the budget for costumed carolers, which is absurd. The singers would come from the high school, and I'm sure we could scrounge up outfits that would work."

"And I'd be happy to help out with buying costumes, if that's the only roadblock," I offered. "Aren't there places that specialize in providing clothes for wild west reenactors and that kind of thing?"

Josie lit up like a Christmas tree. "There are," she said, beaming. "I know that because Willis Dale does cowboy shooting. He'd be able to tell us where to look for things."

"Well, then, that's settled," I said. "Unless Miriam puts her foot down or something."

"She can try," Josie said darkly. "But I'm certain once we get the word out to all the merchants, they'll overrule her. That's the nice thing—everyone in the Chamber gets to have their say, so it's not a total dictatorship...although I'm sure Miriam would prefer that it was."

That was good to hear. I'd joined the Chamber of Commerce after the store was up and running because it seemed like the thing to do, but I hadn't gone to any of the meetings or been involved at all beyond paying my yearly dues. This sounded like another way to give back to Globe...and if I managed to annoy Miriam Jacobsen in the process, all the better.

"I wanted to ask you something," I said next, realizing that Josie had managed to neatly distract me from my real purpose for dropping by that morning.

That comment earned me a tilt of her head, her light blue eyes sparkling. Josie loved it when people came to her for information or advice.

"What happens if my mother and Tom decide they want to sell the Bigelow mansion?"

Her eyes widened. "Are they really thinking about doing that?"

"They haven't said so for sure. But I can tell

they aren't thrilled with what's going on. Still, we can keep this hypothetical for now."

For a few seconds, Josie didn't respond, only shuffled the papers on her desk and placed a completed packet off to one side. Her penciled brows drew together, and she said, "Well, it depends on how eager they are to get rid of the place. To get top dollar, we'd have to put it back on the market…and hope no one's heard about the recent disturbances."

"Don't you have to disclose that sort of thing?"

"Technically, yes." She let out a breath, looking troubled. "And that would be a factor. But if all they want is to unload the property as quickly as possible, then the easiest thing to do would be to go to the buyer they outbid and see if they're still interested."

I ran that possibility through my mind and frowned. "Wouldn't that mean they'd take a hit on the price?"

"Yes," Josie said simply. "The other buyer's offer was quite a bit lower than your parents'. Still, it would make the entire situation a lot less complicated if they were to do that, rather than possibly having the place on the market for months."

I doubted my mother and Tom would find that a very appealing scenario. If they really were going to sell the house, they'd probably want it off their hands as quickly as possible, not hanging like a millstone around their necks for months and months. "Would that even happen, though? My mother made it sound as if the house hadn't been up for sale for very long before she and Tom bought it."

Josie shuffled some more papers, more to give her some cover before she had to reply than because she had much left to do in compiling her packets. "It did sell quickly this first time, yes. But if word gets out that something is wrong with the house, and people start to speculate as to why your parents are turning around and selling it so quickly after buying the place, then that could definitely gum up the works."

I couldn't really argue with that assessment. People tended to get hinky when it came to supernatural goings-on in a house they planned to make their home. And these were no ordinary ghosts, but a bunch of rowdy demons apparently intent on making sure the Bigelow mansion was uninhabitable.

"Who's the backup buyer?" I asked next.

"I don't know," Josie said, and I blinked at her.

"Come again?"

"It was an out-of-state trust represented by a lawyer," she told me. "Believe me, I wanted to know who was behind it, but the lawyer—some slick type from Phoenix—wouldn't give me any information. He told me all I needed to know was that they had the cash on hand to buy the property outright." A pause there, and she gave another sniff. "Apparently not quite enough cash on hand, however, since your parents outbid them. Anyway, they might suffer a small loss in selling to the backup buyer, but at least they'd be out from underneath the house. Did you want me to reach out to the trust's lawyer?"

"No," I said hastily. "My mother and Tom really haven't decided anything yet. I just thought it would be a good idea to find out what their possible options might be." I glanced up at the big brass clock on the wall behind Josie's desk and added, "And now I need to get going. I've got to open the store. Thanks, Josie."

"Oh, it's nothing," she replied. "I really do feel terrible about the situation, because I can assure you, there wasn't even the faintest whiff of the supernatural about the Bigelow house when I went in and took all those photos and did that walk-through video for your parents, despite what Hank and Nora always said about the place being haunted. I can't imagine what happened."

I didn't know, either. The whole thing nagged at me. However, I also didn't know what to do except try to keep digging in the hope that maybe the answer had been there in front of me the whole time.

"Do you have any contact information for the Phoenix lawyer who was representing the backup buyer?" I said. I didn't know for sure where the impulse to ask that question had come from, but I generally tried to trust my instincts.

"Oh, I'm sure I have his card. Just a minute."

She abandoned the open-house packets and opened one of her desk drawers. From there, she pulled out an index card holder, one she'd apparently put to use storing various business cards. After a bit of shuffling, she pulled out a buff-colored piece of card stock with a sound of triumph.

"Here it is," she said, and handed it over to me.

It was a simple card—no logo, just the man's name, address, and a phone number I assumed was in the Phoenix area. "Troy Latimer?"

"That's him," Josie replied. "Slick, big-city type. I have no idea how the trust found him or why they'd decided to buy property in an out-of-the-way place like Globe. I got the feeling they wanted the house for a bed-and-breakfast kind of setup, but Mr. Latimer was pretty tight-lipped about the whole thing."

The man must have been a clam if even Josie

Woodrow couldn't winkle the relevant information out of him. I got out my phone wallet and slipped the business card in with the sad little twenty-dollar bill that floated around with me everywhere, since I rarely used cash and almost always whipped out my platinum debit card for purchases.

"Do you mind if I give him a call?" I asked. "I figure it couldn't hurt to put out a feeler and see if his buyer would even still be interested in the Bigelow mansion. Then I could pass that information on to my mother and Tom."

"Go ahead," Josie told me. "Since you're directly related to the home's current owners, I'm sure he wouldn't mind if you got in touch."

I thanked her and then headed out, knowing I was going to be a few minutes late opening the store. As I went, my mind thrummed.

With any luck, Mr. Troy Latimer might give me some of the answers I was looking for.

12

Divine Intervention

"I'M AFRAID I CAN'T TELL YOU THAT," TROY Latimer said, his tone crisp and no-nonsense— and not leaving much room for maneuvering.

"Why not?" I replied. "I'm not talking about state secrets here. I'm just curious as to whether your client would be interested in a second chance at the Bigelow property."

Since it had been a slow morning so far at Once in a Blue Moon, I'd gone ahead and called the number on the business card Josie had given me. To my relief, I'd actually gotten through to Mr. Latimer rather than shunted off to voicemail or an assistant, but, considering how he seemed determined to stonewall me, that relief clearly had been misplaced.

"I'm afraid that I can't speak to my clients'

intentions," he said. "Especially since you're talking to me in an exploratory fashion and not via direct permission from your parents, the actual owners of the property."

"Not even a little hint?" I asked, desperation clear in my tone.

"Have a good day, Ms. Marx," he said. "If your parents truly decide to sell, feel free to have them reach out to me directly."

And he hung up.

So much for that.

I muttered a curse under my breath and got up from the chair outside the fitting room where I'd sat down to make the call. Even though I loved my shop, with its serene deep blue walls and the gorgeous constellation mural Hazel had painted on the ceiling for me, right then I felt trapped. I wanted to get out, wanted to lock up the place and—

And what? I asked myself, trying to be logical. *You don't have any leads to go on. What you really should be doing is sitting tight and waiting for Tom and your mother to figure out what they want to do with the house.*

Also, feeling trapped was just silly. Once in a Blue Moon was my shop, and I could close it up and sally forth whenever I felt like it. I'd certainly done so plenty of times in the recent past.

The main problem was that I didn't even

know what I'd do with that supposed freedom. Going back to the Bigelow house seemed like a waste of time. What was the point in hearing those screeching demons and smelling that awful stink all over again when I seemed completely unable to get rid of them?

Sasha had called to tell me she was leaving, Brant's ashes in hand. The manager at the Best Western had told her she could leave his car there for as long as she needed, although she said she planned to be back in a few days.

"I just have to wait for one of my friends to have a day off so they can drive me back down here," she said. "But I wanted to call and thank you for everything you've done."

Guilt had washed over me once again. I still couldn't quite stop blaming myself for calling Brant in the first place. If I hadn't reached out to him for help, he'd still be alive.

Since I couldn't change anything about what had happened, I accepted her thanks as best I could and told her to have a safe drive back to Sedona. When I hung up, I tried not to berate myself too much for not doing more. It sounded as though she had a pretty solid group of friends who would help her through this, and I hoped in time the raw edges of her grief would start to get worn down.

In the meantime, I needed to figure out my

next step. I'd called my mother but only got her voicemail. Rather than leave a message—I hadn't even really known why I was calling, except that I'd hoped she might have decided what to do about the house—I just hung up and told myself I'd call again later.

That trip to the Verde Valley was sounding better and better. Too bad it wasn't going to happen for another two months.

But I told myself that just because Troy Latimer had shut me down, it didn't mean I should give up. I pushed the call button for Josie's number on my contacts list.

To my relief, she picked up right away. "Hi, Selena. What can I do for you?"

"Do you know the name of the trust that wanted to buy the Bigelow house?" I asked.

"Not off the top of my head, but I can look it up. Do you mind if I call you back in a few? I have a client in the office with me."

"Sure," I replied immediately, vaguely shamefaced that I'd interrupted an important meeting with one of my wild goose chases. "Whenever you have a chance."

I set the phone down in the little cubby under the cash register where I kept it during the day, and wondered if I should embark on my project to redo the clothing display in the front window, just to keep myself from climbing the walls. However, before I could even begin to summon the energy for that particular task, the bells hanging from the front door jangled as Miriam Jacobsen came sailing into the shop.

Although I thought I maintained a neutral expression, my stomach dropped somewhere around my feet. With the week I'd been having, she was about the last person I wanted to see.

I didn't even have a chance to say hello, because she approached the counter and fixed me with a gimlet stare. "Are you really planning on meddling with our Festival of Lights, Ms. Marx?" she demanded.

Oh, boy. Josie must have mentioned something about my offer to help costume the carolers and kick up the celebration a notch. I summoned a smile and said, "Oh, it was just something I was thinking about. It seems to me that the more we can do to make the event festive, the more people we'll get to attend."

Her nostrils flared. She'd probably been quite beautiful in her youth, with the elegant bones of her face and her ice-blonde hair—now given a peroxide boost, I was certain—and her pale blue eyes. No doubt she'd used her looks to her advantage, and even now, there was something intimidating about the way she was always perfectly put together, hair pulled up into a French twist, always with a matching bag and shoes and outfits that would have worked better for lunch in Beverly Hills than someplace like Globe, where cowboy boots far outnumbered spectator pumps.

"It is already quite festive, I can assure you," she told me. "There is absolutely no need to go to any extra expense for an event that has done perfectly fine all these years without any outside intervention."

My own nostrils wanted to flare at that remark, but I somehow kept my cool. Still, I knew she was implying that I was the outsider here, no matter how long I lived in Globe and how much I contributed to the local economy.

"Sometimes it's good to mix things up a bit," I said sweetly. "You wouldn't want to get stagnant, would you?"

Her eyes narrowed. She always wore perfectly applied false eyelashes, a skill I'd never been able to acquire. "The Festival of Lights is in no danger of becoming *stagnant*," she replied, mouth thinning. "Stay out of it. After all, a heathen like you has no right to be giving advice about a Christmas festival."

And before I could even think of how best to respond to her "heathen" remark, she'd stalked out, letting the door slam behind her with a discordant jangle of the string of bells hanging from the handle.

Of all the….

I told myself to count to ten. Or maybe a hundred.

Who gave her the right to talk to me like that?

Absolutely no one, but since she was already gone, I decided to do my best to calm down and let it go. However, I couldn't help thinking that people like Miriam Jacobsen made it extremely hard to maintain a Zen attitude.

While I was fuming, a man walked into the shop.

He was older, probably in his middle sixties, with iron-gray hair and a firm jaw. The really striking thing about him, however, was the dark suit and white clerical collar he wore.

"Selena Marx?" he asked. His voice was a pleasant tenor.

"Yes," I replied. I knew I sounded a bit hostile, mostly because I couldn't help wondering if some do-gooder citizen of Globe had dispatched him to convert me from my heathen state. Maybe Miriam Jacobsen had already set the dogs on me.

"Hello," he said. "My name is Neil Halloran."

"Brant's friend?" I blurted, recognizing the first name if nothing else. So much for jumping to conclusions. I had to hope he wouldn't hold my earlier dubious tone against me.

"Colleague," he corrected me, but gently. "We worked together on several cases. Sasha Young called me and told me what happened."

It might have been nice if Sasha had mentioned that she'd gotten in touch with Brant's priest friend. Then again, the girl had a lot on her mind…and maybe she'd had no idea that Neil Halloran would show up in Globe out of the blue like this.

"Yes, it was awful," I said. "But…."

I let the word trail off, since what I'd intended to say seemed downright rude.

"But you're wondering what I'm doing here in Globe."

About all I could do was offer him a lopsided smile. "I suppose so. That is, Sasha's already gone back to Sedona. I think she's going to have a memorial service for Brant there."

"Those are her plans, yes," Neil responded. "And I hope to be there for the service. But I'm here because I want to see the house."

"Oh, no," I protested. "It's way too dangerous. After what happened to Brant—"

He cut me off, but so politely that I couldn't really be offended by the interruption. "I understand the risks, Ms. Grant. I have been called to other cases like this, so I know what to expect."

I'm not sure if you do, I thought, but all I said was, "Selena. We're not too formal around here."

"Selena," he repeated. "I really would like to see the place. It's quite possible that I'll be able to cleanse it for you. I understand your family was basically chased out of the place."

Could he really clear out those pesky demons and make it so the house was habitable again? I knew I shouldn't get my hopes up. But....

Well, fortune did favor the bold.

"I was just about to close up for lunch," I said. "Let's go take a look."

———

I stood off to one side, watching Neil Halloran—Father Neil, he'd told me on the drive over, a parish priest from Flagstaff—stand directly in front of the porch steps and stare up at the house. He'd been there for several minutes, although I wasn't sure why. Getting the vibe of the place? Working up the nerve to go inside?

No, that second possibility didn't seem quite right. He exuded the same kind of quiet, steady strength I appreciated so much in Calvin, even though otherwise the two men couldn't have been more different.

Well, I hoped Father Neil was better at catching those vibes than I'd been lately. For me, the house had all the emotional resonance of a bag of Top Ramen.

"Time to go inside, I think," he said. He glanced back at me and added, "You can stay on the porch if you like."

"No, I'm good," I replied. Even though I really didn't want to go back in the house, I also didn't want to act the coward by hanging around outside while a priest walked into the lion's den.

So to speak.

It was just after twelve. The demons had erupted around this same time on two other occasions, so I wondered if they would put on a show for Father Neil today.

Only one way to find out, I supposed.

I mounted the porch steps, then got out the key to the front door and unlocked it. As it swung open, a faint odor of dead skunk and roadkill drifted out.

The priest's nose wrinkled.

"Oh, this is nothing," I said, and stepped inside. "It was much worse the other day."

That was nothing more than the truth. Yes, the stink still lingered, but I could tell it was only the dregs of that initial attack, and not a new blast of the smell. Father Neil followed me, nose still twitching a bit.

"You've never run into olfactory phenomena before?" I asked, hoping I sounded like I knew what I was talking about.

The corners of his mouth lifted slightly. "Oh,

yes, but those were slightly different from this one. Generally, the odors accompanying a demonic attack tend to smell like rotting meat and feces. This is more like dead skunk."

A fine distinction, but possibly a significant one. I didn't really have an explanation as to why the smells here might be different, so I only said, "Most everything happened in the stairwell."

Father Neil nodded and headed in that direction. The house around us was eerily quiet, with only the faint hum of the air conditioning in the background to break up the stillness. I made a mental note to shut it off, or at least push the thermostat up over eighty so it wouldn't be costing my mother and Tom a mint to keep it running. I thought I'd turned it off the last time I was here, but maybe it was preprogrammed to run at a certain temperature, and my fiddling had only changed the settings temporarily.

I followed a few paces behind the priest, figuring that if something decided to push him down the steps, at least I'd be there to catch him, or maybe break his fall. True, he was tall, a little over six feet, but I thought I could probably still manage as long as I didn't lose my cool.

He walked up the lower set of steps, slowly but confidently. But as soon as his foot touched the landing, the noises behind the wall let go, screeching and giggling and wailing. A few seconds later, the pounding started in.

It seemed he hadn't been lying when he'd told me he'd experienced phenomena like this before. His entire body stiffened for just a second, but almost at once he was reaching into his pocket, holding up a cross.

"Behold, the cross of the Lord!" he cried out. "Begone, all evil powers!"

Unfortunately, nothing happened, except the racket inside the walls continued.

"Don't be discouraged," Father Neil said over his shoulder. "It's very rare that the demons are expelled during a first encounter. Releasing their grip on a place—or a person—generally takes time."

I nodded. "Yeah, they weren't too put off by my moon water."

A small smile touched his lips. "No, probably not." Again he reached into a pocket, this one inside the left breast of his black coat. He pulled out a small plastic vial.

"Holy water?" I asked.

"Yes, sometimes it can be more effective than the sign of the cross."

He unscrewed the lid and started flinging the water in all directions, murmuring something in Latin the entire time. A bit of the holy water splashed me as well; I had no doubt that some of the more conservative members of the Globe community would have been surprised to see that the blessed water had no effect on me at all, except maybe to make me glad that it was the middle of summer and I wouldn't have to worry much about going outside with slightly damp hair.

Father Neil was putting on quite a show, but as far as I could tell, the holy water and the Latin chanting weren't having any kind of an effect at all. True, he'd said that it often took a good while to start to wear the demons down, and yet I had to wonder how long he was prepared to keep up the effort.

After about ten minutes or so, the ruckus abruptly stopped. He half swiveled on his black polished shoes and shot me a questioning glance.

"That's how it always seems to work," I told him. "They go on and on…until they stop. There doesn't seem to be much rhyme or reason to it."

"Ah." That was all he said, although I saw how his eyes narrowed, as if he was mentally reviewing the phenomena of the last few minutes and trying to see if they tallied with his previous experiences. Then he tucked the empty bottle that had contained the holy water back in his pocket and asked, "Tell me, Selena—what do you feel from this house? Sasha told me you're a psychic."

I gave a helpless little shrug. "I don't feel *anything*. Or at least, I feel nervous when I walk in here because of what I know I'm facing, but in terms of vibrations or whatever else you want to call them...nothing. I'm still trying to figure it out."

"Interesting." Father Neil paused there for a moment, as though deliberating on what he wanted to say next. "I'm having the same experience. Not that I claim to be psychic in the same way you are, but still, in general when there's a demonic infestation taking place, I can still feel it —a sense of oppression, of dread. There doesn't seem to be anything like that here. And yet...."

"And yet we both heard those noises," I finished for him. "And smelled the stink, even though it's not nearly as bad as it was yesterday. I honestly don't know what to make of it."

Neither did he, apparently. I probably had gotten my hopes up too much in wishing that Father Neil could just fling some holy water around and solve the problem then and there, but still, I really wished we had something to show for our little trip out here.

"Don't despair," he said. "As I said before, these things take time. It might be a good idea to come back at midnight and see what the activity is like then. That's when Brant lost his life, wasn't it?"

"A little after one in the morning," I told the priest. I supposed his idea had some merit, although coming back to the Bigelow mansion in the wee hours of the morning definitely wasn't high on my list of fun things to do with my time. "It could be dangerous, though."

"I'm prepared to face any danger, if necessary," Father Neil said. "And I understand if you don't want to come along. You could give me a key."

That didn't sound like a very good idea at all. Not that I didn't trust him, but I could only imagine my mother's reaction if I let a near-stranger go wandering around in the house without escort. It wasn't so much that she would be worried about property damage or whatnot, just the personal liability if something should happen to the priest while he was here alone.

It wasn't like that sort of thing hadn't happened before.

"No, that's all right," I said quickly. "I don't mind coming back tonight."

"You're sure?"

"I'm sure."

Father Neil didn't look completely convinced, but neither did he try to argue with me. After agreeing that there wasn't much else to see, we headed downstairs and out to my car.

"Where are you staying?" I asked as we were fastening our seat belts.

"The Best Western."

Naturally. He didn't seem like the type to be

staying at the Dew Drop Inn, the shabby little motel on Globe's far western border.

"But I left my car on the street by your shop."

Right. I supposed I should have thought of that. I nodded, and pointed the VW toward downtown. A few minutes later, I parked out front rather than in the parking lot at the back. I didn't know exactly why, except something felt weird about leading Father Neil through the storeroom and into the shop. This way, we were able to say our goodbyes on the sidewalk, and then he headed off toward an older-model Buick parked a few yards away, and I got out my keys and unlocked the shop and let myself in.

Just as I was turning the "be back at" sign around, my phone rang from inside my purse. I pulled it out and looked down at the screen.

Josie.

"Hi, Josie," I said after I'd touched the green button to accept the call. "What's up?"

"I got the name of that trust for you—you know, the one that was trying to buy the Bigelow mansion."

Excitement surged through me, even as I told myself for the umpteenth time that day that I really needed to hold my horses. There was a very good chance the trust would be yet another dead end.

"What is it?" I asked.

"It's called The Lightman Group. I have no idea what that's supposed to mean, though. I went ahead and Googled it, and all I found was that it was incorporated in Wyoming. The names of the officers are all private."

I had to wonder why a trust that had been incorporated several states away was doing business in Globe. It didn't seem to make much sense to me. Then again, just because the trust had been incorporated in Wyoming didn't mean the people involved actually lived there. I was the first to admit that what I didn't know about finance could fit in an area roughly the size of Arizona, but even I knew people often incorporated in states halfway across the country if the rules of incorporation there were more favorable in terms of the fees required or the privacy benefits being offered.

Since she'd sounded almost apologetic about not being able to dig up more information for me, I said quickly, "That's all right, Josie. That's way more than I had to work with a few minutes ago. I'll try to do some digging on my own and see if I can find out anything more."

"All right." She paused and then said, "Do you think there's something to this trust that I missed?"

"I don't know," I replied. "It's just that it keeps pinging my radar for some reason, so I figure I might as well try to find out as much as I can. If it turns out to be a dead end, well, I'll move on to something else."

She agreed that sounded like a good idea, and we ended the call. Afterward, I headed over to the counter, phone still in hand, mind working furiously.

Was it worth consulting the Tarot or my pendulum over this? For some reason, I got the impression my normal methods of divination wouldn't be of much use. I could always call up Grandma Ellen in the crystal ball, but again, I sensed that wasn't a very good idea. Most likely, she'd tell me—as she had in the past—that I had all the clues I needed right in front of me, and it was my job to put them together.

Fine. I'd try a much more earthly way of getting the information I needed.

A quick scan of the sidewalk outside the shop told me no one was loitering in the area, preparing to come inside. I scanned through my contacts list and touched the entry for Calvin's cell phone.

He picked up right away, which told me he was probably in the station and not out in the field, chasing meth heads or rogue cows or whatever else might have called him away from his desk. "Selena? Is everything okay?"

I suppose I should have expected that reaction, since we generally communicated via text when we were working. "Everything is fine," I assured him. "I was just wondering if you could do something for me."

"What is it?" he asked.

Should I be offended that he hadn't said "sure" right away? No, it was smart of him to be cautious, especially since I didn't know if what I was asking was strictly legal.

"Police have access to special databases, don't they?"

I could tell from the way he didn't answer immediately that he was trying to figure out what sort of favor I was asking of him. "Some," he said cautiously. "But it's not like we're the FBI over here or something."

"Could you find out who're the officers of a particular out-of-state trust?"

"Officially, no," he replied. "But…."

"But?" I probed.

"One of my guys here is pretty good at getting around internet security, if you know what I mean," Calvin said. "Give me the name of the trust, and I'll see what he can do."

"Oh, that would be amazing," I replied. "It's called The Lightman Group, and it was formed in Wyoming. But that's all I have to go on."

"That's enough. I don't know when I'll have something for you, because Ben has his own duties that keep him pretty busy, but if we find anything, I'll be in touch."

"Only for that?" I asked, my tone arch.

Calvin chuckled. "Okay, there's a pretty good likelihood I would have been calling you this afternoon anyway. I was wondering if you'd want to come out to my place this evening. I can barbecue."

Two nights together in a row? Over the past few months, we'd seen each other several times a week, but we'd never had dinner on successive nights. Our relationship had obviously moved to a different level, and now I wondered if he wanted it to take yet another step forward.

"That sounds great," I said. "But I'm fine with bringing some stuff over to cook."

"No, you've cooked enough for me. Let me do this for you."

Protesting didn't seem worth the effort. Besides, even though I loved to cook, I was just fine with having my man barbecue for me. It had been a long time since I'd had a grilled meal.

We agreed on seven o'clock, and I said I'd see him there. After I hung up, I belatedly remembered my plans to meet Father Neil at the Bigelow mansion at midnight. No sleepovers at Calvin's house this go-'round, it seemed…if that was even what he'd intended.

Despite that small disappointment, I couldn't

help being cheerful. Calvin was going to have a hacker deputy investigate The Lightman Group for me, and I was going to have an unplanned but very welcome evening at his house that night.

Now all I had to do was vanquish the demons, and everything would be back on track.

13

Bump in the Night

ARCHIE SEEMED REMARKABLY MELLOW WHEN I told him I wouldn't be home that evening. "I suppose you're going to be with that Calvin fellow again," he said. "If you must continue to associate with the man, then you might as well do it at his home rather than yours."

"Thanks, Archie," I said with a grin. "You're all heart."

He only sniffed and headed over to his favorite sunlit spot by the window. Still smiling, I got out a can of cat food and opened it up, then dumped it in his bowl. I hadn't changed for my date at Calvin's house, figuring that a barbecue by its very nature was casual, and so my jeans and sleeveless top would be just fine.

The evening remained clear, with no sign of

any monsoon storms looming, so I popped the top on my Beetle before I backed out of the parking space behind the store. Warm air flowed over me, welcome and somehow calming. Golden late afternoon light burnished the town's buildings as I drove away from Globe and toward San Ramon, although I'd brought along a lightweight sweater just in case. Temperatures around here tended to drop pretty fast once the sun was down, especially on a clear night like this one promised to be.

It felt good to be doing something as prosaic as going over to my boyfriend's house for an impromptu barbecue. I hadn't heard anything from my mother but had decided to let it be for now. Once she and Tom made up their minds, they'd be in touch. And while I was a grown woman and wasn't too worried about my mother scolding me about going back to the Bigelow house when she'd pretty much forbidden it, I figured I might as well stay silent on the subject until I had some real news to report.

Like Father Neil actually succeeding at banishing the creatures who'd decided to park their unholy behinds in the historic mansion.

Because I had the top down, I could smell the scent of grilling as soon as I pulled off the dirt road and onto the gravel lane that led to Calvin's house. I couldn't see him, but smoke drifted up into the air from behind the low adobe building, and so I guessed that was where he must be.

Sure enough, he stood at a big stainless-steel grill that had been shrouded in a black plastic cover the other times I'd been out to the house. The wooden patio table a few feet away already had plates and glasses set out, along with a bottle of wine.

I went over to Calvin and gave him a kiss on the cheek. "That smells amazing," I said. "What're we having?"

"Grilled tri-tip, corn on the cob, and finger-ling potatoes on skewers," he replied.

A quick glance down at the grill confirmed the menu. "I had no idea it was going to be so gourmet. I figured we'd be having burgers."

He grinned, teeth flashing white in the warm early evening light. "No, you're worth more than that. And this isn't so complicated. Actually, what you're seeing here is pretty much my entire cooking repertoire, so I hope you enjoy it."

"I know I will."

A flip of the big piece of meat sitting on the grill, and then he closed the lid and led me over to the table. "Here's to dining *al fresco*," he said, and picked up one of the stemless plastic wine glasses on the table so he could fill it. After handing it to me, he poured more wine into the second glass and touched it to mine.

"Definitely," I replied. The wine was good, a big fruity zinfandel that would be great with the grilled meat.

He really couldn't have picked a better night for a barbecue. Did Calvin's people have their own weather sense? Was that why he'd known we needed to take advantage of this lovely clear evening?

Maybe. Whatever the reason, I was glad to be able to sit down and enjoy the warm air, the scent of dry grass and sun-heated juniper that surrounded us with their soothing, aromatic perfumes.

"A priest came into the shop this afternoon," I said—I'd already decided it was better not to mention Miriam Jacobsen's incursion, since I knew Calvin had a pretty low opinion of her— and his brows lifted.

"Is that the beginning of a joke?"

"No," I replied, although I couldn't help smiling at his question. "I guess Father Neil worked with Brant Thoreau on cases like this one, and Sasha Young called him. I know she was just trying to help me out, but I don't know if it's such a good idea to get someone else involved with the mess at my parents' place."

Calvin sipped some zinfandel. "Did you tell him that your mother told you to stay away?"

"Well…."

The brows went up again. Since it was Calvin, he didn't launch into accusatory comments right away, but only sat there and waited for me to incriminate myself.

I wouldn't lie to him. "Actually, I went over to the house with him earlier today."

"Selena—"

"It was fine," I said quickly. "I mean, the demons were at it again, but nothing really happened. Father Neil got to hear them, and he tried a few things to get them to go away."

"Did any of it work?"

"No," I replied before adding, "but he told me it often takes a few tries to banish demons. It's not like spraying for ants, you know."

"Actually, ants are pretty hard to get rid of, too," Calvin said.

Since the corners of his mouth were quirking, I knew he was teasing me…sort of.

"True," I said. Should I tell him I was planning to meet Father Neil at the mansion at midnight? I guessed Calvin wouldn't be too happy to hear about that particular scheme. On the other hand, we'd promised to be honest with each other, and I didn't think hiding things from him was a very good idea. "We're going back to the house tonight."

At once, his brows drew together again. "You aren't."

"We are. He wanted to see if there were any differences in the demons' behavior at midnight as opposed to during the daytime."

For a few seconds, Calvin remained silent. His long brown fingers tapped against the side of his glass, and so I had a feeling he was less than happy with me and was trying to think of the best way to tell me this midnight visit was a terrible idea and that I needed to call it off.

Finally, he said, "I really think you should let this go. I don't want to sound callous, but the house is your parents' problem, not yours. You've done what you could."

Since that was pretty much the same thing my mother had told me, I couldn't muster any terribly convincing arguments to counter what Calvin had just said. Honestly, I didn't know for sure why I kept pushing so hard on this, except that I didn't like unanswered questions, and my instincts kept telling me there was more here than met the eye.

I told him, "It's not as if I'm going there alone."

"You're going with someone you just met and don't know anything about."

Clearly, Calvin's experience questioning

witnesses had made him very good at exposing all the weaknesses in a particular argument. I sipped some wine, trying to think of the best way to respond.

"He's a priest," I pointed out.

"He *says* he's a priest," Calvin countered. "Did he show you any credentials?"

"Well, no," I admitted. "He was wearing a clerical collar, though."

At that remark, Calvin shot me a disbelieving look, as if he couldn't believe I could possibly be that naïve. Voice even, he said, "You can buy those online."

Really? It wasn't exactly the sort of thing I would have even thought of, considering my experience with members of the clergy was pretty limited. "Maybe, but Brant mentioned Neil to me before he died, although he didn't say he was a priest. The two of them obviously knew each other, or Sasha wouldn't have sent him down here. I suppose there's just the faintest possibility he could be some kind of impostor, but I don't see the point in pretending to be something he's not. Besides, I didn't get any bad vibes off him, or see anything in his aura that would tell me he was anything except who he claimed to be."

Which was the truth. I hadn't made an effort to will Father Neil's aura into being, but I'd caught a flicker or two from it and saw only cool, reassuring blue, not the muddy orange of deception.

Calvin listened to all this, expression still skeptical, although he at least didn't try to interrupt. When he spoke, his voice was as calm, as measured, as always. "I don't want anything to happen to you, Selena. One man has already died in that house."

"I know," I replied. And believe me, I did. Even though Sasha had reassured me that none of this was my fault, I knew it was going to be a while before I could shake off my lingering guilt from Brant Thoreau's death. "That's why I wouldn't go there in the middle of the night if I were going alone. But Father Neil has experience with these sorts of things. It'll be fine."

"Maybe I should come with you," Calvin suggested, and I shook my head.

"I'm not going to drag you out in the middle of the night for this," I told him. "For one thing, you don't have any experience with the supernatural—"

"Well, except the whole coyote shifter thing," he cut in, now looking faintly amused.

"That's not the same," I said severely. "That's just part of who you are. It's not like dealing with things that go bump in the night."

"I wasn't aware they were your specialty, either."

Although I wanted to argue that point with him, I knew he was partially right. I wasn't a medium or an exorcist. I had communicated with Lucien Dumond's ghost, and I had regular convos with my dead grandmother in a crystal ball, but it wasn't as if this was the sort of thing I focused on. Even so, I still had a lot more experience than Calvin.

"It's more mine than yours," I said, and he let out a resigned breath.

"You're right. And since you're a grown woman who can make her own decisions, I guess I can't really stop you. I just want you to know that I don't like it."

"Duly noted," I replied. "And we'll be careful. No worries on that point."

A nod, and then he got up to flip the tri-tip again. That seemed to put an end to the discussion, although I could tell he wasn't too happy with me.

So much for a romantic evening together.

Because of the friction between us, I didn't stay late at Calvin's house. He kissed me goodbye and told me he'd let me know when and if his deputy dug up anything about The Lightman Group, but I could tell he was still troubled by my decision to go back to the Bigelow mansion at midnight.

Since I knew I'd be heading out again in a few hours, I didn't bother to get ready for bed when I got home. I set an alarm on my phone for 11:30 in case I fell asleep watching TV, and then plonked myself down on the couch to wait it out. Archie seemed a little surprised that I was home by nine, but he must have sensed something of my mood, because he didn't say much, only curled up in the armchair and dozed off.

I did pretty much the same thing from my spot on the couch, and was glad I'd set that alarm. When my phone began buzzing, I started awake and stared, bleary-eyed, at the screen for a moment before I remembered why I was supposed to be getting up.

Right then, I thought that maybe Calvin had been right in trying to dissuade me from carrying out this particular plan.

But I didn't have much choice. I suppose I could have called Father Neil—he'd given me his cell number, just in case—and yet that seemed like a cowardly thing to do. And after all, I'd been present for several of these demon rampages, and although they could be frightening enough, nothing had actually happened to me during any of them.

So I went in the bathroom and splashed some

water on my face, then put on fresh lip gloss and pulled my hair back in a scrunchie. Thus readied for demon-fighting, I picked up my purse and headed out.

At that hour, hardly anyone was out and about in Globe. A party town, it was not. I only passed one other vehicle on my way out to the Bigelow mansion, and that was just as I was leaving the downtown area. Once I started to cut through the hillside residential areas, I didn't see a single soul.

No sign of Father Neil's Buick as I pulled up near the garage and came to a stop. Well, the clock on my dash said it was 11:54, which meant I was a little early. I'd checked my phone before I left and didn't have any missed texts or calls, and so I had to assume this midnight meeting was still on.

I slung my purse over my shoulder and headed toward the front porch, figuring I might as well wait for the priest there. If he was running late, I'd just sit down on one of the wicker chairs on the porch. Maybe waiting in my car would have been more comfortable, but at least this way, I'd be able to spot him the second he pulled on to the property.

The night breeze was pleasantly cool, faintly scented with the fragrance of the numerous rose-bushes blooming in the garden only a few yards away. Sitting on the porch like that, I could almost forget why I was here…or what lurked in the house behind me.

A few minutes ticked by. I reached in my purse and looked at the screen. 12:05.

Had Father Neil decided to bail on me?

Although I'd only known the guy for a single day, he didn't seem like the type to ghost a person, especially over something this important. I suppose it was possible he'd forgotten to set an alarm, or had car trouble or something. But if that was the case, wouldn't he have called or texted?

The phrase "doomed venture" floated through my mind, although I told myself I was being melodramatic. Five minutes late didn't constitute a catastrophe in anyone's universe.

A rhythmic thumping sounded deep inside the house. It sounded as if the demons were at it again…and here I was, sitting on the porch.

Another glance at my phone.

12:10.

Well, if the good father couldn't be bothered to call me, then I'd just have to call him.

I navigated to the contact I'd entered the day before and touched the button to connect the call. His phone rang four times, and then I heard, "Hi, you've reached Father Neil Halloran's voicemail. Please leave your name and phone number and the reason why you're calling, and I'll get back to you as soon as I can."

A beep followed, and I hesitated, wondering whether it was even worth my time to leave a message. After all, either he was coming to meet me, or he wasn't.

But then I gave a mental shrug and said, "Hi, Father Neil. This is Selena. I'm at the house, but I don't know where you are. I'll wait a bit longer, but after that I'm just going to head home. Thanks."

Once I was done, I replaced the phone in my purse, feeling vaguely foolish. Right then, I couldn't quite ignore the sensation of overwhelming futility.

The pounding kept going inside the house. Didn't the demons know they didn't have any kind of an audience?

Or maybe they could sense I was out on the porch.

A shiver wriggled its way down the back of my neck. I found I didn't like that idea very much.

But it was silly to stay here. I needed to pack it in and go home. Whatever was going on with Father Neil, I couldn't guess, but that didn't mean I should keep sitting on this porch, listening to the chirping of the crickets in the yard and the faint sighing of the wind in the trees.

Then again....

Why not go inside and take a peek? If nothing else, observing the phenomena again would let me figure out if there was any kind of baseline, so to speak, or whether the demons mixed it up depending on their mood.

And yeah, I know. Dumb idea. Don't go into the haunted house and all that. But I was getting kind of tired of being stymied at every turn.

At least I had my running shoes on.

Now resolved, I stood up and unlocked the front door, then let myself in. I'd left an accent lamp in the living room on, just so the house wouldn't be completely dark. Its reassuring glow showed me that nothing looked out of place. To the eye, the mansion was calm.

My ears were an entirely different matter. The pounding and screeching and laughing continued, just as before. Listening to it, I found myself getting angrier and angrier. How dare they? This house wasn't theirs—it was supposed to be a place of peace and beauty.

They needed to get out.

I stomped over to the stairs and pounded my way up to the first landing. "Shut up!" I yelled. "Stop it! Pick up your toys and go home!"

This entirely unprofessional tirade was met with about the reaction I should have expected— i.e., absolutely no change whatsoever. Gritting my teeth, I went over to the wall and thumped it with my fist.

"Stop it!"

Again, no diminishment of the noise or its intensity. I smacked the wall again, then paused.

What the heck?

Something about the wallpaper had felt strange. I paused and got out my phone, turning on the flashlight function so I could get a better look. The stairwell had its own light fixture, but I hadn't turned it on, and I was too far away from the accent light in the living room to see much more than large shapes.

Yes, that was definitely an obvious seam in the paper, one which didn't quite match the pattern, as if that one piece had been hung quickly and sloppily. I hadn't noticed it before since the floral design was fairly busy, typically Victorian. And although I suppose it was possible it had always been like that, I got a hinky sensation again, as if there was something else going on here besides badly patched wallpaper. Beneath my fingertips, the paper felt cool and oddly damp. Surely wallpaper that had been up for decades shouldn't feel like that?

My fingertips slipped under it, began to pull. Yes, it felt like the paper was starting to come up —and not in bits and pieces, like old, dry wallpaper that had been there for fifty years or more, but in one solid sheet.

What the…?

Something hard connected with my back, pushing me toward the stairs, and I stumbled and dropped my phone. I flailed as I tried to catch my balance, but it was too late. My Keds slipped on the top step, and I went down hard, rolling and rolling until I hit the bottom.

Then my body took mercy on me, and I blacked out.

14

Hazard Pay

"Selena!"

Calvin's voice, urgent. I cracked an eyelid and winced at the light shining in my eyes. Everything *hurt.*

"Are you all right?"

"Define 'all right,'" I muttered.

"Can you feel your fingers? Your toes?"

"Unfortunately, yes."

His arm slipped under me as he helped me up to a sitting position. I blinked, and realized I was at the base of the stairs, with lights blaring all around. Except for the heavy beating of my heart, the place seemed utterly quiet. The demons appeared to have checked out for the evening.

"What happened?" I asked.

Calvin was positively grim-faced, mouth and jaw taut. "I was hoping you could tell me that."

He handed me my phone in its wallet case. "I found this on the landing. Good thing you keep your phone in that case—it looks like it survived the fall."

"Better than I did." I put my hand up to my head, which was pounding like the demons that lived in these walls. Near the back of my skull was a tender spot, probably the beginning of a lump. Still, I knew I'd been very, very lucky. "What are you doing here?"

His mouth tightened even further. "I was worried about you, but I knew you'd be annoyed with me if I just showed up here without being asked. Still, I had a bad feeling about the whole thing, so I started listening to my police scanner."

I didn't bother to ask why he had a police scanner at his house—it probably made sense for him to be able to stay on top of things even when he wasn't physically at the station. "And?"

"And I heard that Father Neil had a car accident on his way over here. Someone T-boned him as he was crossing Highway 60."

Shock flared through me. "Is he okay?"

Calvin nodded. "He's got a couple of cracked ribs and a concussion, but it's nothing life-threatening. They're keeping him in the hospital overnight for observation."

No wonder he'd never showed up. And thank

the Goddess that he'd be okay. "Did they catch who hit him?"

"No. The person driving the other car abandoned the vehicle and fled on foot. And the car had been reported stolen just a few hours earlier, so there's no way to connect it to the driver. They're checking for fingerprints, just in case, but it doesn't look good."

My head was swimming, and I was pretty sure it wasn't just because of the tumble I'd taken a while earlier. "Do you think he was hit on purpose?"

Still looking grim, Calvin shook his head. "It's way too early to know that. A perp fleeing the scene of an accident isn't that unusual. With any luck, Henry Lewis and his people will track him down."

I didn't respond. While Chief Lewis and I were far from friends, I couldn't argue that he seemed to be competent. And since the accident had happened squarely in Globe, there was no question of Calvin being involved with the case at all.

"Can you stand?" he asked next. "I want to get you out of here."

My head ached, and I had a feeling I was going to be covered in bruises, but it didn't feel as if I'd suffered anything except superficial injuries. "I think so."

With Calvin's strong arm supporting me, I laboriously got to my feet. For just a second, the room swam around me, and I clung to him.

"Are you okay?" he asked, his grip on me tightening a bit, as if he was worried I might collapse without him to brace me.

"I'm fine," I assured him. "Just a little dizzy."

"You might have a mild concussion," Calvin said. "Maybe I should take you to the hospital."

"No," I said, then tried to smile so my protest didn't sound quite so flat. "I just want to go home. I'm sure I'll be fine after a good night's sleep."

"Any blurred vision?"

"No," I replied. "I think I just got up too quickly."

He sent me a dubious look but didn't say anything else, only helped me cross the foyer to the front door and out onto the porch. Once we were outside, I dug the key to the door out of my pocket and handed it to him, and he locked up for me.

"You can leave your car here for the night," he said as we made our way to his big white Durango, parked not too far from my VW Beetle. "I'll come back with you tomorrow to get it."

"That's not necessary—" I began, but he shook his head.

"You shouldn't be driving. And you know the car will be perfectly safe here."

Since the demons' rampages had been restricted to the interior of the house, I had to admit he was probably right on that point. "Okay," I said meekly.

He helped me up into the passenger seat and then went around the front so he could slide behind the wheel. We drove in silence for a few minutes before he said, "You really shouldn't have gone in there by yourself."

"I know," I replied. "It was a stupid thing to do. I was just feeling so…frustrated. I wanted to feel as if I was accomplishing something. All I accomplished was to get pushed down the stairs."

That remark made him swivel his head toward me, dark eyes wide with worry and something else, something that looked like blazing fury. "Someone *pushed* you?"

"I—" I paused there, remembering that I wasn't just talking to my boyfriend, but to the man who was the head of the San Ramon tribal police. True, this wasn't his jurisdiction, although, judging by the flash of anger I'd seen in his face, I had a feeling he didn't care much about such niceties when his significant other was involved. "I don't know," I said lamely. "I lost my balance and fell. I think maybe I bumped my shoulder against the bannister and it just felt like someone pushing me."

This feeble story didn't seem to convince him, because he said, "Selena, if someone pushed you, then we're talking about an attempted murder investigation."

"I know," I said. "Or I mean, I get it. But it all happened so fast, and everything was so muddled, that I can't really remember for sure what happened."

His fingers tightened on the steering wheel, but he remained silent, as if he'd realized that pushing me on the subject wasn't going to accomplish anything. And I couldn't say for sure why I was trying to muddy the waters—or why I didn't want to tell him about the weird wallpaper I was investigating when those unseen hands had shoved me—only that my sixth sense was telling me this was a clue I needed to follow up on my own.

We were quiet the rest of the way to my place. When we got there, he insisted on helping me up the stairs and into my apartment. I didn't argue, mostly because I was pretty sure I couldn't have managed those steps on my own.

"Are you sure you're still doing all right?" he asked as I eased myself onto the couch. "Any more dizziness? Blurred vision?"

I raised a weary hand. "None of that. I'm sure

I'll be all sorts of interesting colors tomorrow, but I'm okay. I'm tougher than I look."

"Apparently." He bent and laid a gentle kiss on my forehead, and I breathed in, instantly feeling better. There was something solid and reassuring about Calvin, something that made me think nothing truly bad could happen while he was around. For a second, he hovered near the sofa, clearly uncertain as to what he should do next. "Do you want me to stay?" he said. "I can sleep on the couch."

"You don't need to do that," I told him. "Really, I'm fine. Besides…what time do you have to be at work?"

"Seven."

I generally didn't even lift my head from my pillow before seven-thirty, and so I knew I didn't want him rattling around the front room while I was trying to sleep. Again I said, "I'm fine. I'm just going to rest here for a bit, and then I'll go to bed. And you need to get to bed, too, if you have to be up that early."

He glanced toward the door and back toward me. "If you're sure…."

"I'm sure," I said, my tone firm. "You need your sleep. And I'll text you as soon as I'm up. Okay?"

"Okay," he echoed. He stood there a moment more, then bent and kissed me again, a very gentle touch of his mouth against mine. "You took a big risk tonight, Selena."

Since he was right, I didn't bother to argue. Besides, my head was starting to throb again, and I didn't want to make it hurt more by going back and forth with Calvin all over again. "I know. It was stupid. But I'm all right."

He only shook his head, then touched my hand before heading to the door. Once there, he paused and said, "I'll wait for your text," before letting himself out.

For a minute or two, I remained on the couch, trying to gauge whether I actually had the strength to walk from the sofa to the living room, or whether I should just crash where I was and pull up the afghan I had draped over one arm of the couch and call it a night.

But no, sleeping on the sofa would only make me that much more cramped and achy and generally unhappy with life. I gritted my teeth and made myself limp to the bedroom, and prayed I'd feel better when I woke up.

"Better" was probably a relative term. However, even though I ached all over and could see the bruises that had formed on my arms and legs overnight, my head wasn't hurting quite as much as it had been when I went to bed, so I doubted I had a concussion, even a minor one.

Well, my mother had always said I was hard-headed.

Moving slowly, I shuffled into the kitchen and put the kettle on the stove, hoping that a cup of strong Darjeeling might make me feel a bit better about life.

I'd just finished wincing my way through bending down to put some food in Archie's bowl when the cat appeared at the entrance to the kitchen. "Wild night?" he asked in sour tones.

"You missed all that?" I responded, straightening with some effort as I reached around to massage the small of my back. Well, maybe a long, hot shower would help with some of the aches and pains.

"I was sleeping."

Of course he was. "I took a tumble down the stairs at the Bigelow mansion last night."

Archie's little pink nose twitched. "I told you not to go there."

You and everyone else, I thought. But because I didn't see any reason to withhold the truth from my feline roommate, I said, "Someone pushed me."

That comment earned me a slight tilt of his head. Rather than respond with questions about my well-being, however, he only said, "The same person who pushed the man from Sedona?"

"Maybe. They came up behind me, so I didn't see anything."

Archie walked over to his bowl, glanced into it, and then deigned to take a few mincing bites. After he was done chewing, he said, "It sounds like someone has something to hide."

I'd been thinking pretty much the same thing. The memory of the rough edge of the wallpaper I'd found flashed into my mind. I had been just about to start tugging at it when my attacker had pushed me away.

What was under that wallpaper?

I glanced at the clock. Nearly nine. A little too early to call my mother, but once I'd eaten and showered and gotten dressed, it would be past ten. I'd get in touch at that point.

Because I had a feeling I should probably get permission before I started my own little remodeling project on her stairwell.

———

"You want to do what?" my mother asked. From somewhere behind her, I could hear the annoying hum of a distant leaf-blower. That was one thing I really liked about living in Globe—I hadn't seen a single one of those damn things in use anywhere around here.

"I want to pull back the wallpaper in the stairwell," I said. "I think there's something odd going on in there."

When I'd called, I'd confessed to going back to the house but had carefully avoided any mention of the attack. I was fine, except for some bruises that were probably going to display a stunning array of colors over the next few days, and I didn't see the point in getting my mother upset over what had turned out to be nothing.

Okay, attempted murder wasn't "nothing." But I was more interested in getting to the bottom of the demon problem at the Bigelow mansion.

"I really don't like the idea of you going in there by yourself," my mother told me, her reluctance obvious in every syllable.

"I won't be going by myself," I reassured her. "I'll have my friend Hazel with me."

That was nothing more than the truth. I'd already gotten in touch with Hazel and asked if she could come with me on my fact-finding mission. In fact, I'd also asked her if she could bring Chuck along, because I figured having six feet, two inches of solid cowboy muscle on standby couldn't hurt.

But she'd told me he was going down to Willcox for the day for a cattle auction, so that put the kibosh on my clever idea. Still, I thought that going back to the mansion with a friend in tow—and going there in broad daylight—would make the whole situation a lot safer.

"We-ell…." Although my mother still sounded dubious, I knew when she hesitated like that I'd begun to wear her down.

"It'll be fine," I said. "Really."

A long pause. Then a sigh breathed its way out of my iPhone's speaker, and she said, "All right. To be perfectly honest, Tom and I were thinking about taking down that wallpaper anyway. It's awfully busy."

I had to agree with that assessment. While the floral paper might have been correct for the home's period, it was a little headache-inducing.

"Then it sounds like this will work out for everyone," I told her. "And don't worry—Hazel and I will be out of there at the first sign of trouble."

Another of those pauses. "All right. Just… please be careful, Selena."

I promised her I would, and ended the call. The clock ticking away on the mantel told me it was twenty minutes after ten, which meant Hazel would be over shortly.

That gave me enough time to call the hospital and inquire after Father Neil. They patched me through to his room right away, which told me he must be doing all right.

Sure enough, he sounded pretty cheerful when he picked up the phone, although some of that cheer faded after I told him I'd gone inside the mansion without him.

"That could have been dangerous," he said, sounding worried.

Oh, it was, I thought, although I didn't say the words out loud. Instead, I replied, "It was fine. The demons were doing their usual thing, though. Well, minus the smell."

He chuckled. "That must have been a relief."

"I'm sorry about your accident, though," I went on. "What happened?"

A pause. "It was odd. I was leaving the parking lot of the hotel and was about to turn onto the highway when someone came barreling down the side street and plowed right into me. I don't know how they couldn't have seen my car—a Buick is pretty hard to miss."

I couldn't argue with that statement. "Who was driving the other car?"

"I don't know. A man, but he took off running almost immediately. The police told me the car was stolen."

Car theft was pretty rare in Globe. Maybe that was because most of the town's residents tended to drive their vehicles until they dropped in harness, and so the few cars that were actually worth stealing were too distinctive to make the crime worth the effort involved.

"It was definitely a man driving, though?" I asked.

"Yes. The lighting wasn't that good, of course, since it was eleven-thirty at night or so, but I could tell it was a man with dark hair. Not too tall, but those were the only details I was able to notice."

The world was full of dark-haired men who weren't overly tall, so that particular detail probably wasn't going to help the police track down the guy. "Well, I'm glad you're all right," I said. "Do you know how long you're going to be in the hospital?"

"Oh, they're going to release me later today," Father Neil replied. "I have a mild concussion and a couple of cracked ribs, but it's not enough to keep me here. My car is totaled, though, so someone from the Phoenix diocese is driving over here to pick me up and take me back where I can rent a car."

"I'm so sorry about all this—" I began, but he cut me off before I could go any further.

"What happened certainly isn't your fault, Selena," he said. "And I came down here to Globe of my own free will. I'm just sorry I couldn't be of more help to you."

Honestly, I didn't know how much help he

could have been even if he'd made it to our midnight meeting. Once again, that feeling of barking up the wrong tree was back, and I thought that having a priest on this case maybe wasn't the best plan of action anyway.

I murmured something noncommittal, and after making sure Father Neil's friend from the diocese would be there to take him from the hospital back to the hotel so he could get his things, I hung up and looked at the time.

Nine twenty-five.

Taking advantage of the five minutes I had left before Hazel showed up, I went into the bathroom to perform a quick mirror check and make sure I wasn't betraying any obvious signs of my tumble of the night before. Luckily, I'd managed to avoid banging up my face, and I was wearing a lightweight yoga hoodie and jeans, which hid the bruises that had started to bloom along my legs and arms. Maybe not the best outfit for August in Arizona, but it was better than trying to explain why I looked like I'd taken up kickboxing as a hobby.

I'd just finished pulling my hair back into a scrunchie—after checking to make sure I didn't have any betraying bruises or scrapes on my neck —when someone knocked at the door. I hurried out of the bathroom to answer the knock, and saw

Hazel standing just outside, a red plastic bucket in one hand.

"I thought you could use these," she said, holding up the bucket so I could peek inside. Stowed within were a metal scraper and a spray bottle of water. "I had them lying around from when I first moved into my house here and I had to scrape off all this horrible wallpaper from the 1970s."

"Oh, that's perfect," I told her. "The wallpaper at the Bigelow mansion felt as though it was going to lift pretty easily, but this will definitely help if it decides to be stubborn."

She looked pleased, but the faint smile she was wearing slid away soon enough. "You're really sure you want to do this? Maybe it would be better to wait until Chuck gets back from Willcox."

I honestly didn't know why I was in such a hurry, but what I did know was that if my instincts were telling me to do something, then I needed to get it done. My mother had seemed cooperative enough, and yet I had a feeling the reluctance I'd heard in her voice partly stemmed from the realization that she and Tom had already made up their minds about the house, and she thought I was going to a lot of work for nothing.

Another reason for haste was Calvin. He was smart enough not to outright forbid me to do something, but I doubted he'd be too happy once he found out I'd gone back to the Bigelow house after taking a fall that could have been fatal. We both knew all too well that those stairs had proved deadly just a few nights earlier. Better to do this while he was safely busy at work.

"No, I don't think we need to wait for Chuck," I said quickly. "Believe me, I'm ready to cut and run at the first sign of trouble. This honestly shouldn't take too long."

"Famous last words," Hazel returned, but since her mouth quirked a little as she spoke, I got the feeling she was kidding…sort of.

The two of us went downstairs and out to the spot where my car was parked behind the building. After Hazel had stowed her bucket of supplies in the back seat, I pulled out and headed off toward the east edge of town and the Bigelow mansion.

We'd been driving for a couple of minutes when Hazel remarked, "What's with the hoodie? It's supposed to be in the low nineties today."

I thought furiously. "Oh," I said, "my mom left the A/C in the house cranked way up, and I still haven't figured out how to reset the thermostat. You can hang out on the porch if it gets too cold."

Hazel lifted an eyebrow at my explanation but didn't say anything else. And honestly, it wasn't a total lie. The air conditioning had been left on at a much lower temp than was strictly necessary, and although I'd eyeballed the thermostat, I hadn't fiddled with it. The previous owners had installed ducting and dual high-efficiency cooling units, and the thermostat that had gone along with the system was one of those overly complicated ones with different settings for times of day and days of the week. Thank the Goddess that the one in my own apartment was simple and only asked that you push a button to adjust it upward or downward as required.

The day was almost as bright as the previous one, although a few ominous, mushroom-shaped clouds on the far horizon indicated that it didn't intend to stay clear. No biggie; I planned to be safely back at the store before any monsoon weather erupted.

I parked in nearly the same place I had the day before, right next to the spot where the flagstone front path touched the edge of the gravel driveway. Hazel and I got out, and she pushed the seat up so she could retrieve her bucket from the back. Thus armed, we headed for the front porch.

Everything looked quiet. I couldn't hear any sounds coming from within, which had to be a good sign. True, we were here at an off hour, at a time of day when the demons hadn't previously made their presence known. I hoped that meant I'd be able to work without getting interrupted, but—as I'd assured Hazel—I was ready to bolt at a moment's notice. The night before, I'd just barely managed to escape serious injury. I definitely wasn't going to press my luck today.

Since I'd held on to the key, I only needed to extract it from an inner pocket of my purse and unlock the door. It swung inward, and Hazel wrinkled her nose.

"What is that *smell?*"

"Demon mischief, I guess," I said. "It was a lot stronger the other night."

"Ugh."

"You can keep the door open and wait here," I suggested, but she shook her head.

"No, it's probably better if we stick together. Besides, I spend half my days inhaling linseed oil and turpentine. I can handle it."

The set of her jaw told me she had no intention of staying meekly by the door while I went further into the house and risked attack by demons. Her loyalty cheered me, so I didn't bother to protest, only headed toward the stairwell, then flicked on the miniature chandelier that hung above the landing.

It flared to life, illuminating the gaudy floral pattern of the wallpaper. That same bright light clearly showed the spot where I'd begun to pick at it the night before, the edge now starting to curl slightly.

"Do you need this?" Hazel asked, proffering the bucket she held.

"I'm not sure," I replied. "Let me pull at it a little bit and see what I can find."

I climbed the stairs while she followed, casting furtive glances in every direction as if she expected a whole army of demons to emerge from the walls and start attacking us.

To tell the truth, I was sort of on edge, too. It was more unnerving than I'd thought it would be to have the house so deadly silent, the only sound the faint whisper of the air conditioning in the background. And the air in here really was downright cold, so that made my story about the hoodie a bit more plausible.

I grabbed the edge of the wallpaper and pulled. To my relief, it came up in one continuous sheet, pulling away from the plaster beneath with a weird sucking noise that sounded somehow sticky.

Hazel looked on, eyes wide with shock. "It shouldn't do that."

"Shouldn't do what?"

"Come off in one piece like that. If this wallpaper is as old as the house—or even if the previous owners hung it years ago—it should be really dry and come off in patches...and only then after a lot of coaxing." She came closer and put her fingers on the section of wall I'd just revealed. "This still feels damp."

"You mean it's new?"

"Sure feels that way."

Now it was my turn to stare at the wall in consternation. "How long does wallpaper take to dry?"

Hazel shrugged. "It depends on a lot of factors. But we've been damper than normal here, thanks to all the thunderstorms, so it could take up to a week or even longer."

A week. My parents had closed the deal on the house six days earlier. But what did that mean, exactly?

Frowning, I kept pulling on the wallpaper, tearing it off in huge sheets. Hazel caught them as I yanked them down, and then set them over to one side of the landing.

They revealed a clear patch in the plaster, about two feet wide and five feet in height, starting at the baseboard. For a second or two, I could only stare at it.

My friend spoke next, sounding hesitant. "Do you think there was something wrong with the house, so they fixed it quickly and then put up new wallpaper, hoping your parents wouldn't notice?"

That seemed like the most plausible explanation. Shady, yes, but all sorts of underhanded stuff went on during real estate transactions. However, my instincts were telling me that there was more going on here than a simple ploy to conceal some bad plumbing.

I set my hands on my hips and said, "I think we need to tear down this wall."

15

Household Demons

FOR A SECOND OR TWO, HAZEL ONLY STARED at me. Then she seemed to find her voice and said, "You want to do *what?*"

"I need to get inside this wall and see what's going on in there."

That declaration earned me an emphatic head shake. "Selena, this house is more than a hundred years old. That's plaster and lath you're talking about, not drywall. You'd need a crowbar to open it up."

Right. I hadn't even stopped to think about that aspect of the situation, since I'd be the first to admit I wasn't exactly what you could call an expert when it came to old houses. I quickly ran down the list of items in my car that might help in this particular situation and came up with exactly one. "Would a tire iron work?"

Her eyes widened even further. "You're seriously going to tear up this wall with a tire iron?"

Good question. My mother had told me it was okay to pull down some of the wallpaper, but that wasn't exactly the same as giving me *carte blanche* to demo the wall using automotive tools. Well, better to ask forgiveness than permission… and obviously I would pay whatever it took to repair the wall and hang new wallpaper, or have it painted if that's what she and Tom would prefer.

"Yes," I said. "Hold tight."

I all but ran down the steps and out the front door, then grabbed the tire iron from the Beetle's cargo compartment. When I returned, Hazel had moved closer to the wall and was running her fingers over the plaster.

"This is all new, too," she told me. "That's probably part of the reason why the wallpaper wasn't curing properly. The glue couldn't set while the plaster underneath was still damp."

I might not have known much about home repairs, but even I knew that you didn't go to all that work unless there was something massive you wanted to hide. This felt like a lot more than just trying to conceal bad plumbing or termite damage.

For a second or two, I stood there, hefting the tire iron in my hand, wondering if I actually had the guts to start hacking at the walls of my mother and Tom's historic house. Wouldn't it be better to come back with someone who actually knew what they were doing?

Obviously, Hazel sensed my hesitation, because she said, "Maybe you should call Brett. I'm sure he would look at this for you."

Yes, Brett the handyman, Josie's nephew, was probably much better suited for this kind of task than I was. However, because he was so good at what he did, he was much in demand and generally not the sort of person you could call to drop everything and show up to demo a wall.

"He would," I agreed. "But I doubt he's available."

Before I could lose my nerve, I lifted the tire iron and swung it into the wall. Hazel made a muffled exclamation, but she didn't try to stop me, only stepped out of the way so she wouldn't get hit by any flying bits of plaster.

Strangely, it felt good to be hacking at the wall with the tire iron, as if each blow was my way at getting back at the demons who'd killed Brant Thoreau, terrorized my mother and Tom, and sent me tumbling down the stairs. After the fifth or sixth blow, an entire section of plaster gave way, leaving a gaping hole in the wall.

Inside was...well, I had to stare at it for a minute before my brain could start to put the pieces together.

"Is that a *boombox?*" Hazel asked incredulously.

It was. I hadn't seen one in years, but that was definitely a big black portable stereo inside the wall, placed on a small stool. A black cord snaked away from the device and was plugged into a naked outlet. Just beyond the boombox—and partially toppled over by collapsing plaster—was an odd-looking contraption like something out a Bugs Bunny cartoon. It consisted of several articulated arms with mallet heads at the end. As far as I could tell, it had been set up so the mallets would hit the wall at varying intervals, although with it knocked out of place, I couldn't be completely sure. Both items were connected to another device I didn't recognize, but which I guessed turned them off and on somehow. Maybe RF signals, like a radio-controlled toy car?

Spurred by a sudden thought, I leaned into the gap in the wall and reached out to touch the Play button on the boombox.

"Don't!" Hazel said, and I glanced back at her, startled, finger still suspended above the boombox's controls. Looking sheepish, she added, "I mean, you don't want to disturb any fingerprints that might be on there. That's all."

Right. I doubted anyone who'd put the boombox in the wall had done so out of the goodness of their heart. I got a tissue out of my purse and shielded my finger with it as I pressed Play.

At once, a horrible shrieking and moaning and giggling erupted out of the boombox. Hazel gasped, and I took a step backward in fright before I realized exactly what all those noises were.

The demons.

Or rather, what someone had wanted us to believe were demons. I stared down at the odd contraption with the mallets, and guessed it had been designed to create the awful pounding that made it sound as if something was trapped inside the wall, trying to get out.

No wonder I'd never gotten a feeling of evil here, even though all my physical senses had been telling me that something was very wrong with this house. And no wonder Brant had held back from definitely commenting on the subject, had kept doing his best to gather more evidence. There hadn't been any demons at all…only someone who'd desperately wanted us to believe there were.

Someone who was willing to kill to keep up the charade.

From behind me, Hazel said, "So…it was all a fake?"

"Looks like it," I replied. I returned the tissue to my purse and pulled out my iPhone. Feeling grim, I took photos of the items we'd located inside the wall, and shot some video as well, making sure I caught a good chunk of the *faux* demonic moans and groans.

"But…why?"

"To drive Tom and my mother out, as far as I can tell," I said. "They did a pretty good job of it, too."

But who would be willing to resort to this kind of subterfuge…and why?

"You'd better call Chief Lewis," Hazel said next.

Right. If this had been a simple case of mischief, I wouldn't have wanted to get the police involved. But whatever was going on here, apparently it was important enough to the person or persons behind the scam that they were willing to commit murder to make it work.

"Okay," I said, and tried not to let out a sigh. I knew I had to do the right thing, but I really, *really* hated having to deal with Henry Lewis.

The police chief stuck his head inside the wall. Even though I couldn't see his face, I got the impression that he was frowning a mile a minute. A second later, demonic howls and shrieks erupted from the boombox.

"Well, damn," he said, then shut it off with a press of one gloved finger.

"You see?" I replied. "Someone was deliberately trying to scare my parents out of this place."

"Who?" he asked, and I shot him a disbelieving look.

"How would I know?" I said, doing my best not to sound too offended by such a ridiculous question. "They don't even know anyone around here. It's not like they have enemies."

Chief Lewis appeared to ponder that statement for a moment, then gave a reluctant nod. "True…I suppose." Before I could object to that insinuation, he went on, "We'll dust for fingerprints, see if we can find any evidence that might lead us to who put this stuff inside the wall. Your parents are back in California, right?"

For the umpteenth time, I reflected wearily on how quickly news traveled in Globe. Then again, I'd told Josie they were gone, and that was pretty much all it took.

"Yes," I said. "They're safe."

Chief Lewis looked almost satisfied by that reply. "Good. Tell them to stay in California. I'd say it's a safe bet that whoever put these things here is the same person who pushed Brant Thoreau down the stairs."

I'd made the same deduction, so I didn't argue. Instead, I rolled up my sleeves and showed off the impressive array of multicolored bruises on my forearms, garish in the light from the chandelier overhead. Standing over to one side, Hazel let out a startled sound.

"And they tried to do the same thing to me last night," I said.

Henry Lewis's eyes narrowed. "You were pushed?"

I nodded. "Yes. Luckily, all I got was a bunch of bumps and bruises. But I definitely felt someone push me, although I couldn't see who it was."

He absorbed that statement, then said, "Well, you should still come to the station and file a report. Makes it easier to file additional charges against the person who did this, whenever we track him down."

While I wasn't exactly keen to get all official about what had happened to me, I understood his position. I'd been lucky...and Brant Thoreau had not. We needed to make sure the perpetrator was punished for all his misdeeds.

"Okay," I said. "I'll go over there after we're done here."

"You can go now," he replied, gray eyes starting to look a little flinty. "There's nothing else you can do here. I'll lock up and bring you the key once we're done inspecting the crime scene."

I wished I could protest. But Henry Lewis was being pretty mellow, all things considered, and I didn't want to set him off.

"Sure."

I looked over at Hazel and gave a little nod, and she followed me down the stairs and outside.

"Why didn't you tell me?" she asked once we were off the porch.

"Tell you what?"

"That you were attacked here last night?"

I stopped in the middle of the flagstone path. The sun shining down on us was almost uncomfortably warm, but it felt good.

Someone had deliberately tried to get my mother and Tom out of this house, and they hadn't cared who they hurt in the process. That knowledge made me cold inside, a chill I wasn't sure even the August sun could completely dispel.

"I didn't want to freak you out," I said.

Hazel crossed her arms. "I'm not the kind to 'freak out,'" she replied. "And I think you know that as well as anyone. Don't you think I would've wanted to know it could be dangerous coming here?"

"You already knew that," I pointed out, somewhat disingenuously, and she lifted an eyebrow.

But then she let out a breath, appearing to relent. "True…I suppose. Still, I don't like it when people keep things from me."

"I'm sorry," I said, and meant it. The last thing I'd wanted to do was upset her. It was just that the same instinct that had guided me to be here this morning was also the instinct which had told me I really didn't have anything to worry about on this particular go-'round.

And that had turned out to be the truth, thank the Goddess.

"Okay." Hazel glanced over at my car. "Guess we'd better get over to the police station."

Since a deputy took my report and not Chief Lewis, the whole experience wasn't too bad. Afterward, Hazel and I adjourned to Olamendi's, figuring we'd earned some margaritas and tacos after what we'd found in the Bigelow mansion. I debated texting Calvin and then decided I'd much rather tell him the story in person, instead settling for a quick message.

Some stuff went down today. Dinner tonight?

He'd responded with a quick "yes" and no questions. For all I knew, he'd already heard a chunk of the story over his police scanner.

"Who would want to do that to your parents?" Hazel asked after taking a big swallow of mango margarita.

"I don't know." I drank some margarita as well, although mine was a classic on the rocks with an extra splash of Cuervo on top. Luckily, the restaurant was walking distance from my store…not that I was sure I even wanted to go in after lunch. Maybe it would be better to keep the store shut down, just in case Chief Lewis had additional questions for me or needed me to go back out to the mansion. "But it's got to have something to do with the other people who wanted to buy the place."

"Do you know who they are?"

I shook my head. "Unfortunately, no. That is, Josie told me it was a trust of some sort, and she gave me the name, but I haven't been able to find out much more than that. Calvin said one of his guys was going to look into it for me. I don't think it was top priority, though."

"Well, maybe it should be now," Hazel remarked as she reached for a tortilla chip and dunked it in some of the restaurant's yummy, bright green cilantro salsa. "Considering these people are apparently okay with murder if it serves their agenda."

Maybe that was why Calvin hadn't been especially chatty when I texted him. He'd already instructed his hacker deputy to get on the problem and didn't want to discuss the situation in depth until he had more information to give me.

We had plans to get together for dinner, but right now, seven o'clock felt awfully far off.

"I'm sure they're working on it," I said. "I

guess about all I can do now is sit tight and see what develops. And I need to call my mom and let her know what's going on."

"What do you think she's going to say?"

Good question. My mother was not the sort to lose her cool easily, but I thought even she might be taken aback to learn the Bigelow mansion was important enough to someone that they were willing to commit murder over it.

I suppose that was the one thing I couldn't quite wrap my head around. Yes, it was a beautiful, historic house, but that still shouldn't have been sufficient motivation.

Clearly, I was missing a piece of the puzzle... and I thought I'd better do what I could to figure out what that particular puzzle piece actually was.

Since Hazel was watching me, obviously expecting an answer, I shrugged and said, "I don't know. I mean, I doubt she'll be happy, but I don't know whether this new information will make her want to dig in her heels about keeping the house, or whether she'll be happy to let it go because it's turning into way more trouble than she expected."

My friend shivered a little and reached for another tortilla chip. "Personally, I'd want to get rid of it. I couldn't imagine living in a house with that much baggage."

While I completely understood Hazel's position on the issue, the situation with my mother and Tom was a little more complicated. They'd never planned to make the Bigelow mansion their full-time home, and so maybe they were willing to put aside all the awful events of the recent past in order to have a historic house as their base of operations while they were visiting me in Globe a couple of weeks out of the year.

I only said, "I get that," and reached for a chip of my own. While I was glad of the food and the margarita, I really wanted to get home so I could do a little digging of my own…hedgewitch style.

———

Since I'd popped in to feed Archie after I was done at the police station and before I went out to lunch with Hazel, he wasn't too annoyed with me when I slipped into the apartment and headed to my office.

However, he still couldn't let me pass by without making a comment. "Aren't you supposed to be at work?"

"I'm the boss," I replied in the overly sweet tones I often employed when talking to my cursed cat. "One of the perks is that I get to set my own hours."

"Hmph," he said, tail waving in disapproval. "Back in my day, people had a work ethic."

"They had girdles, too," I replied. "Not everything about the good old days was all that great."

As I'd hoped, the mention of foundation garments was enough to get Archie to leave my office in disgust. He stalked off to the living room, clearly done with me.

Good. I preferred to do this sort of thing alone.

Just to be safe, I closed the door to my office. Then I went over to my altar.

The crystal ball there glimmered in the sunlight streaming through the window, and I hesitated. My Grandma Ellen had been a lot of help in the past when it came to solving these sorts of puzzles, and I wondered if I should just go straight to her for assistance. After all, the problem I faced now involved both her daughter and her granddaughter, and maybe that would make her more willing to lend a hand…so to speak.

But I hesitated. When Lilith Black was murdered, my grandmother had flat out told me I had all the necessary facts on hand to find her killer, and so she wasn't going to tell me who the guilty party was, since I was perfectly capable of ferreting out that information on my own. There was every chance she'd do exactly the same thing in this instance.

Probably better to give it a go with some other

methods first before I pulled her away from her afterlife cabana boys, or whatever she did with her time when she wasn't dispensing advice from inside my crystal ball.

I reached for my Everyday Witch tarot cards, figuring that since this particular problem involved a house, a deck which focused on more domestic matters might be a better choice than some of the others. After shuffling it several times and focusing on the mystery of the boombox and the strange mallet contraption in the walls of the Bigelow mansion, I pulled three cards, figuring a simple spread was the best place to start.

Well, so much for that idea. I basically got what I called "minor arcana muddle," a batch of cards that didn't seem to have any relevance to the particular issue I needed clarified. Still, I tried pulling three more sets of three before I decided the Tarot cards just weren't going to work.

All right, time to move on.

I got out my fluorite pendulum and let it swing in the air for a moment as I focused once again. Then I held it over the oracle board I had sitting on the altar.

The pendulum swung again, seemingly at random…and then its movements became more precise, picking out three letters.

A-L-L.

Okay, this was not the time to get all metaphysical on me. I suppose the argument could be made that since all of mankind was connected, it had something to do with Brant's murder and the strange contraption inside the walls of the Bigelow mansion, but I thought that was something of a reach.

Maybe the pendulum needed to hear my intentions before it could provide a more concrete answer.

"Who put the boombox inside the wall?" I asked. "Who pushed Brant Thoreau down the stairs?"

Once again, the pendulum moved.

A-L-L.

Sigh. Sometimes divination could be a real pain in the ass.

I looked over at the crystal ball, sitting innocently on its stand of wood carved into sacred crescent moon shapes. Hopefully, Grandma Ellen wouldn't be too annoyed about me bothering her with my latest mystery.

Even as I set down the pendulum, though, I got a sudden flash.

No.

In this case, it felt like the universe telling me that bothering my grandmother wasn't the way to go.

"Then what?" I asked plaintively.

My mind's eye showed me the stairwell in the Bigelow mansion, complete with the gaping hole I'd started with my tire iron and which Chief Lewis and his men had extended even further so they'd have easy access to the boombox and the strange little pounding device that had accompanied it.

"I'm supposed to go back to the house?" I asked.

No direct answer, but I had the feeling I'd hit the nail on the head with that question…and I thought I knew why. Henry Lewis had the items they'd found inside the wall locked up as evidence. That didn't mean I couldn't go over there and touch the wall itself, or the bare electrical outlet inside the wall, clearly placed there to power the "demonic" devices. My powers of psychometry had helped me before, revealing the whereabouts of Lilith Black's killer.

I had to hope they'd come to the rescue this time, too.

Feeling slightly encouraged, I went to my office door and opened it. Sitting outside on the carpet runner in the hallway was Archie, who shot me a sardonic golden-eyed glance.

"Talking to yourself now?" he asked. "Some people say that's a sign of madness."

"Well, if that's the case, that ship sailed a long time ago," I responded blithely. "Anyway, I'm off to the Bigelow house. Try not to get in any trouble while I'm gone."

His tail twitched. "I should be the one telling you that," he said. "Considering you're the one who fell down the stairs the last time you were there."

"I didn't fall—I was pushed," I pointed out.

"Even worse."

Under other circumstances, I might have been more hesitant to return to the scene of the crime. In this case, I thought I should be safe enough. "Well, I'm sure whoever is responsible is giving the place a wide berth now. We know the demons were a fake, and Chief Lewis is examining the evidence we found. It's only a matter of time before he tracks down the perpetrator."

If Archie had been human, he might have lifted an eyebrow. As it was, he tilted his head ever so slightly and then said, "Your funeral," before stalking off into the living room.

I refused to accept his bleak view of the situation. My instincts were telling me to go back to the house, and I doubted my psychic abilities would override my own sense of self-preservation.

At least, I had to hope they wouldn't.

A quick check to make sure the cat's water bowl was filled, and then I grabbed my purse and headed out the door. By that point, the drive to the Bigelow mansion was so familiar that I really didn't have to think twice about which streets to take or where to turn. Soon enough, the big house with its warm and friendly paint scheme of green and brick red and gold came into view, and I headed up the gravel driveway and parked in my usual spot near the path.

No monsoon clouds loomed today, and it was bright and sunny, warm verging on hot. I adjusted my sunglasses as I got out of the car and headed up the walk to the front door, then retrieved the key from an inner pocket of my purse.

The door swung open. By this point, the stink inside had subsided to a dull murmur, sort of like a hotel room where someone had smoked but the cleaning staff had done their best to get the place sanitized. I wondered what the trickster had done to make that terrible smell. Containers of skunk spray sitting in the air ducts? It probably had to be something more controlled than that, though, because otherwise the stench would have continued to foul the place.

Whatever the reason, I was just glad I could walk around the house without feeling like I was going to gag.

The curtains were still pulled back the way Henry Lewis and his team had left them the day before. I was glad of that, glad of the bright sunshine pouring in and brightening the place. Now the Bigelow mansion looked cheerful and welcoming, rather than the typical Victorian haunted house that played a cliché role in way too many horror movies.

Not so cheerful was the big hole on the landing. Seeing it now, with the place as well lit as it was, I realized what a godawful mess we'd made. Of course, it could be repaired, but it was going to take a lot of work.

Well, I'd deal with the fallout from the excavation later. I'd already mentally resolved to pay for the repairs, considering I was the one who'd taken a tire iron to the wall in the first place.

I was just about to step into the hole and start touching the exposed frame when my phone pinged from inside my purse.

Calvin.

Ben managed to dig up some info, his message ran. *You're not going to believe this, but The Lightman Trust was established by Miriam Jacobsen. I don't have much more than that right now. I'll keep you posted.*

I stared down at my iPhone's screen in shock. Miriam Jacobsen? The dragon lady who ruled the Chamber of Commerce with an iron fist? Why in the world would she be mixed up in something like this? I didn't know much about her—and was glad of that, considering my run-ins with her had been anything but cordial—but I knew that she seemed to live a comfortable life in her big house up near the top of Bailey Street, living off investments and the small honorarium the Chamber paid her. She seemed like the last person in the world to get her hands dirty in some kind of real estate scheme.

"Ahem."

The throat-clearing had come from the foot of the stairs. I emerged from the hole in the wall and shoved my phone back in purse.

Standing at the base of the steps was a stocky dark-haired man who looked like he was probably in his late fifties. He shot me a friendly grin, showing white teeth that seemed sort of at odds with his overall rumpled appearance, and said, "I came over to take a look at the damage."

"'Damage'?" I repeated stupidly.

He cocked his head toward the gaping hole behind me. "Uh, the damage to the wall."

"Oh, right." Man, my mother moved fast. Maybe Chief Lewis had gotten in touch with her and let her know that they were done investigating the opening in the wall, and so she'd decided to get going with repairs. So, did that mean she planned to hang on to the place? I went down the steps and extended a hand. "I'm Selena Marx. My parents are the owners."

Another smile. "I know," the man said as he took my hand and shook it. "I'm Al Loomis."

It was like a blinding flash of monsoon lightning—the pendulum spelling out "A-L-L," the truth itself flowing from his fingers to my own.

Al Loomis had put the boombox and the mallet device in the wall. And no doubt it had been those same hands that had pushed me down the stairs…had pushed Brant Thoreau to his death.

I don't know what my face looked like right then. My expression must have changed—and not for the better—because a look of almost regret passed over his blunt features.

"I'm really am sorry about all this," he said. "But Miriam said to get it done, and I will."

And he reached behind him to pull a gun out of the waistband of his jeans.

16

It All Comes Out in
the Wash

I FROZE. IT WAS ACTUALLY THE FIRST TIME I'D ever seen a gun in person, since I'd never had any desire to go shooting for recreation, and I generally didn't hang out in the sorts of places where guns were brandished on a regular basis.

And yet, here I was.

The gun itself was shiny, with a longish barrel. The opening at the end of that barrel looked big enough to swallow me whole.

"You really don't have to do that," I said, my voice all breathy and tight, not at all like my own. "I won't tell anyone."

Al's shoulders lifted infinitesimally. He wore that same almost sad expression. "I'd like to believe that, but since you've already helped track down two murderers, I don't have much reason to believe you wouldn't do the same to me."

Fair point. Still, I could tell he was reluctant to pull the trigger. Pushing someone down the stairs in the darkness was one thing. Having to shoot them point-blank as they stared at you and asked you not to hurt them was something else entirely.

My mouth was drier than the sun-baked hillsides surrounding the town. "But…why?"

He waved with the gun toward the wall, and I flinched. It would be just my luck for the thing to go off accidentally and take me out at the same time. "Miriam wanted the house. There've been some developers nosing around who thought this location would be just perfect for a new resort, but Hank and Nora would never agree to sell it to someone who only wanted to tear it down. Miriam figured she'd buy the place and then sell it off. Easy peasy." Al frowned then. "Except then your parents decided they had to have it."

"And so there was a bidding war," I said.

"Yeah." He reached up to scratch his head, mussing his gray-flecked dark hair. "Turned out your parents had deeper pockets, and Miriam had to drop out, since she was putting up her own money, figuring she'd get it back tenfold after she sold the place to the developers."

While I was relieved that Al seemed inclined to keep talking—maybe he felt the need to get all this off his chest before he buried a bullet in me—I couldn't quite figure out why Miriam had played the middleman in all this. "Why didn't the developers just buy the house themselves? Obviously, they must have the money to do it."

"Because Hank and Nora put a clause in their contract that the property had to be preserved as it was, with no major changes," Al explained. "Miriam had to buy it first, and then she could sell it without any of those restrictions."

"Right," I said. The gun had drooped a little, was now pointing roughly at my bellybutton rather than my chest, but I had a feeling it would do just as much damage there if it went off. My gut clenched, but I tried to sound calm as I went on, "And so when she lost the bidding war for the house, she decided instead to try to scare my parents into selling the place."

He nodded. "It seemed like an easy enough plan. Miriam got the idea from Hank and Nora's stories about ghosts, and thought conjuring demons would make the house even less attractive."

"'Stories' about ghosts?" I asked. Maybe that wasn't the most important thing to be worrying about right now, but the words slipped out anyway.

The question got me half a smile. "The place

wasn't really haunted. Hank and Nora always thought it should be, though, so they made up a bunch of stories about a ghost. Anyway," he went on, "Miriam figured you would put your own two cents in, since you were into all that woo-woo stuff and would convince your parents this wasn't a good place to live." Al's heavy brows pulled together as he added, "We didn't think you'd be pulling in all sorts of outside experts."

"And so you pushed Brant Thoreau down the stairs," I said, even as I marveled a bit at how calm I sounded.

"No," Al replied at once, looking indignant. "I mean, I realized I probably would have to, because he was listening to the wall through a stethoscope and would probably figure out soon enough that the sounds were fake, since I ripped them off from the *Conjuring* movies and some other stuff. But just as I was approaching him, Brant startled at a noise or something, and he lost his balance and fell."

This story didn't relieve me as much as I would have liked it to. Yes, Brant's death had apparently been an accidental one, but Al Loomis was still standing there with a gun pointed at me.

I almost asked whether he was going to deny pushing me, then decided it wasn't worth the effort.

"And Father Neil?" I inquired.

Now Al looked abashed. "Miriam told me to stop him from coming out here, so I did. But man, I'm going to be going to confession for that one for years."

Did they have confession in prison?

Probably better not to ask.

"Look, Al," I said, trying to sound as gentle and persuasive as I possibly could, "it really sounds like Miriam was behind all this, and you're just someone who got dragged into her schemes. I think what we need to do is go talk to Chief Lewis and let him—"

I broke off there, because the gun had lifted at those words and was now pointed back at my chest.

"No cops," Al said. "Henry Lewis isn't going to care that this was Miriam's idea. He's still going to arrest me for being an accessory to murder. So, the only real solution is to get rid of you. Luckily, there's lots of desert here in Arizona. A body can go missing for years."

My heart began to thump painfully in my chest. How unfair was it that I was going to get murdered just as everything was going so well between me and Calvin? And over something so stupid as a real estate deal?

"I can call my mother and tell her to sell for

whatever price Miriam wants—" I began, but Al only shook his head.

"That won't work. They'll know who was involved. The only way to make this right is to make sure you disappear."

I tried to swallow past the lump in my throat. Anything to make my mouth a little less dry. How was this possible?

His finger tightened on the trigger, and I tensed.

The front door opened, letting in a blaze of sunlight. "Al?" came an incredulous voice.

Standing in the doorway was Brett Woodrow, Josie's handyman nephew. Probably, she'd sent him over here to take a look at the hole in the stairwell and start working up an estimate.

Never in my life had I been so glad of Josie's busybody nature.

Al half turned, startled. I knew I had just this one chance.

And hey, it worked in the movies.

Without pausing to think, I flung myself at him, catching him in the midsection. He stumbled, and I elbowed him in the ribs. His fingers still grasped the gun, however.

Damn it.

Time to fight dirty.

I kneed him in the groin, and he howled in agony but didn't loosen his death grip on the gun.

Fine. Desperate times called for desperate measures.

The second I buried my teeth in his wrist, Al let out a startled shriek. A millisecond later, the gun dropped from his hand to the floor and slid a few paces away.

Through some miracle, it didn't go off.

"Get it!" I screamed at Brett.

To my relief, he didn't waste time asking questions, only hurried over to the spot where the gun had come to rest and picked it up. An audible *click* a minute later told me he must have reengaged the safety.

Seeming to sense the tide had turned, Al shoved me away and bolted for the door. But Brett stuck out his foot, and the other man crashed to the wood floor like the proverbial ton of bricks.

"Hold him there," I called out.

Thank the goddess, Brett didn't even hesitate. He and Al were about the same height, but Brett was probably twenty-five years younger than the guy and was much more agile. A few seconds later, he had my assailant pinned down by means of some kind of complicated-looking maneuver.

"High school wrestling," he said briefly in reply to my startled glance.

Perfect. I glanced around the room, knowing I needed to find something to tie up our perp until the police could get here. Extension cords—the trusty standby I'd used to tie up Globe's two previous murderers—seemed to be in short supply. However, the living room's heavy velvet curtains were held back by silk ropes with tassels on the ends. I hurried over to a window and removed one of the tiebacks, then brought it over to my rescuer.

"Here you go," I said.

Brett took the rope from me and used it to bind Al's hands behind his back. He struggled a bit, but there was something halfhearted about his movements, as if he knew the jig was up and there wasn't much he could really do except lie there and accept his fate.

Once he was secured, I got out my phone and dialed 9-1-1. The woman who picked up sounded a bit surprised when I told her we had the person responsible for the fake demons at the Bigelow mansion tied up and ready for transport by the authorities, but she promised me someone would be out right away.

In Globe, that wasn't a false promise. Our police department wasn't exactly overburdened with crimes it needed to investigate, so I knew a deputy would be dispatched immediately. Maybe even Chief Lewis himself, if he happened to be in the station when the call came in and not out driving around town and looking for miscreants the way he often did.

After I ended the call, Al muttered, "Miriam is going to kill me."

Brett sent me a sideways look. "Miriam? Miriam *Jacobsen?*"

"Sounds that way. She wanted to buy this property so she could sell it to developers for ten times what she paid."

That revelation made him give a disgusted shake of his head. "Anything for a buck." Then he cheered up a little and added, "On the bright side, I suppose this means she won't be president of the Chamber anymore."

Probably not. I had a feeling it might be kind of difficult to conduct that kind of business when you were locked up for fraud and attempted murder. Or at least, accessory to attempted murder.

I was just glad that the demons had turned out to be a definite fake.

———

"Sorry I missed the excitement this time," Calvin said.

I reached for my glass of sauvignon blanc and took a sip. We were sitting on his patio, enjoying the warm early evening breezes and the delectable smell of teriyaki-glazed chicken skewers cooking on the grill. After I'd called Calvin to get him caught up on all the day's events, he'd suggested that I come by after he got off shift, and I, safe in the knowledge that both Al Loomis and Miriam Jacobsen were behind bars, figured I'd earned the evening off.

"If you'd been there, Chief Lewis would have been ticked off," I replied. "Not your jurisdiction."

"Still." Calvin was silent for a moment before adding, "You were insanely lucky to have Brett show up like that."

Oh, didn't I know it. Maybe that was why the universe had sent me back to the house...it had known I wouldn't be in danger. Not really, even though it had given me a heck of a scare.

"Thank goodness for Josie butting into everything," I said. "When I talked to my mother, she told me she gave Josie the go-ahead to have Brett go over and take a look around. But if he'd been even a few minutes later...."

I let the words trail off. Yes, I'd gotten Al Loomis talking, but sooner or later, he would've gotten tired of our little chat and pulled the trigger. Or maybe, when the moment came, he wouldn't have had the nerve. However, I was glad

I hadn't been forced to rely on a sudden attack of his conscience to keep me safe.

Anyway, he was still looking at five to ten for pulling the gun on me, and a lot more for all the other little escapades he'd been involved in, including trespassing on the property to install his fake-demon setup inside the wall, as well as violations of something called Title 13, since he'd installed hidden cameras all over the house to keep track of my mother and Tom's comings and goings. And while Miriam was loudly proclaiming her innocence, no one seemed inclined to believe her. Calvin's deputy Ben had provided the electronic trail that proved she was The Lightman Group's one and only officer, and from there it wasn't too difficult to follow the breadcrumbs and see that she'd been involved every step of the way. She might still be kicking up a fit and complaining about the conditions in the county lockup—Josie had dropped that little tidbit when she stopped by to get the full story from me—but it was pretty apparent that Ms. Jacobsen's reign in Globe was now over.

It also helped that Al had pretty much thrown her under the bus and told Chief Lewis the entire thing was her idea, and that she'd egged him on with the promise of a big payout once the development company bought the property from her for many times what she'd paid for it.

There was definitely no honor between those two thieves.

Calvin leaned over and brushed his fingers against my arm, and a happy little warmth flowed through me. Funny how just the slightest touch from him was enough to make me all gooey inside. "But Brett wasn't too late. You're safe, and the mystery of the Bigelow mansion demons has been solved."

"And my parents are planning to come back in a week or so after Brett has all the repairs done and gets some new paint up," I said, relaying what my mother had told me earlier that afternoon during a lengthy phone call. "So, that's definitely all's well that ends well."

"I'm glad they're not giving up the house." Calvin drank some of his wine, then pushed himself up from his chair so he could go tend the chicken skewers.

Watching him, I found myself smiling, so glad to be there in the sunlit tranquility of his back-yard. Yes, there had been mayhem and deceit—and some pretty nasty property damage—but at the end of it, the bad guys were in jail where they belonged, and Globe was peaceful again.

I suppose I'd have to wait and see how long that lasted....

Selena's adventures will continue in *Perpetual Potion*, releasing in October 2021.

Be sure to sign up for Christine Pope's mailing list and join her Facebook group so you won't miss out on any of the fun!

Also by Christine Pope

HEDGEWITCH FOR HIRE

(Mystery/Paranormal romance)

Grave Mistake

Social Medium

Household Demons

Perpetual Potion (October 2021)

Jingle Spells (December 2021)

THE WITCHES OF WHEELER PARK

(Paranormal romance)

Storm Born

Thunder Road

Winds of Change

Mind Games

A Wheeler Park Christmas

Blood Ties

Healing Hands

Wishful Thinking

Smoke and Mirrors (January 2022)

PROJECT DEMON HUNTERS*

(Paranormal Romance)

Unquiet Souls

Unbound Spirits

Unholy Ground

Unseen Voices

Unmarked Graves

Unbroken Vows

THE DEVIL YOU KNOW*

(Paranormal Romance)

Sympathy for the Devil

Charmed, I'm Sure

A Wing and a Prayer

THE WITCHES OF CANYON ROAD*

(Paranormal Romance)

Hidden Gifts

Darker Paths

Mysterious Ways

A Canyon Road Christmas

Demon Born

An Ill Wind

Higher Ground

Haunted Hearts

THE WITCHES OF CLEOPATRA HILL*

(Paranormal Romance)

Darkangel

Darknight

Darkmoon

Sympathetic Magic

Protector

Spellbound

A Cleopatra Hill Christmas

Impractical Magic

Strange Magic

The Arrangement

Defender

Bad Blood

Deep Magic

Darktide

Rising Dawn

THE SEDONA FILES*

(Paranormal Romance)

Bad Vibrations

Desert Hearts

Angel Fire

Star Crossed

Falling Angels

Enemy Mine

TALES OF THE LATTER KINGDOMS*

(Fantasy Romance)

All Fall Down

Dragon Rose

Binding Spell

Ashes of Roses

One Thousand Nights

Threads of Gold

The Wolf of Harrow Hall

Moon Dance

The Song of the Thrush

THE GAIAN CONSORTIUM SERIES*

(Science Fiction Romance)

Beast (free prequel novella)

Blood Will Tell

Breath of Life

The Gaia Gambit

The Mandala Maneuver

The Titan Trap

The Zhore Deception

The Refugee Ruse

STANDALONE TITLES

Hearts on Fire

Taking Dictation

Golden Heart

Night Music: A Modern Reimagining of The Phantom of the Opera

Ghost Dance: A Sequel to Gaston Leroux's The Phantom of the Opera

Flight Before Christmas

About the Author

USA Today bestselling author Christine Pope has been writing stories ever since she commandeered her family's Smith-Corona typewriter back in grade school. Her work includes paranormal romance, fantasy romance, and science fiction/space opera romance. She makes her home in New Mexico.

Don't miss out on any of Christine's new releases —sign up for her newsletter today!

Christine Pope on the Web:
www.christinepope.com